DESTINY'S DELTA (SPECIAL FORCES: OPERATION ALPHA)

DELTA TEAM 3, BOOK TWO

BECCA JAMESON

Dear Readers,

Welcome to the Special Forces: Operation Alpha Fan-Fiction world!

If you are new to this amazing world, in a nutshell the author wrote a story using one or more of my characters in it. Sometimes that character has a major role in the story, and other times they are only mentioned briefly. This is perfectly legal and allowable because they are going through Aces Press to publish the story.

This book is entirely the work of the author who wrote it. While I might have assisted with brainstorming and other ideas about which of my characters to use, I didn't have any part in the process or writing or editing the story.

I'm proud and excited that so many authors loved my characters enough that they wanted to write them into their own story. Thank you for supporting them, and me!

This series is special to me as the five authors writing in the Delta Team Three series took a team that I introduced in *Shielding Kinley* and made them their own.

READ ON!

Xoxo

Susan Stoker

ACKNOWLEDGMENTS

I want to thank Susan Stoker for all her hard work putting this series together. I'd also like to thank all the authors in this group for such a fun ride. Lori, Lynne, Elle, and Riley—you all rock! It was so much fun working with all of you. What an amazing series this turned out to be.

Nori's Delta by Lori Ryan
Destiny's Delta by Becca Jameson
Gwen's Delta by Lynne St. James
Ivy's Delta by Elle James
Hope's Delta by Riley Edwards

PROLOGUE

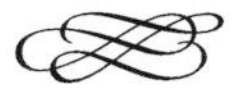

Today was definitely the worst day in Trent Dawkins' eighteen years. For one thing, it was a Friday night and he'd stayed home all evening. After graduating from high school last week, he'd seen almost no one besides his parents and, occasionally, his brother, Sean. Trent was leaving for the Army in a few days, but for some reason, the thought of running around acting like a fool with his friends hadn't appealed to him.

Hell, partying hadn't appealed to him for several months, actually. Not since Sean had started dating their next-door neighbor, Destiny. Not since Trent had swallowed his tongue and given Sean his blessing. Not since he'd started lying to himself and everyone around him as if he didn't care if his brother dated the prettiest, sweetest girl in school—the one Trent had had his eye on since he was old enough to be interested in girls.

Sean was also leaving for the military soon. He'd enlisted in the Navy. And he'd been out with Destiny nearly every agonizing night for weeks.

Trent hadn't even joined his parents in the living room to watch television. He'd had a bad feeling about this night all afternoon. A premonition that the universe was not on his side today.

He'd been lying on his back on his bed, tossing a ball up in the air and catching it for hours to keep from pacing and fidgeting, when he heard the car pull up.

Trent caught the ball and closed his eyes. His heart raced as the front door opened and voices filled the house. Excited voices that rang out, thundering in his head, making his stomach clench.

And then his mother squealed in delight.

Yep. The world stopped spinning, just as Trent anticipated.

Sean hadn't spoken to Trent about his plans, but Trent was a smart guy. He certainly couldn't claim to be shocked.

His twin brother and best friend in the world had asked the cutest, nicest girl Trent had ever known to marry him.

Trent couldn't bring himself to rise from the bed. He felt his life shatter into a thousand little pieces. He couldn't catch his breath. All he could do was roll onto his side as a tear slid from his eye and swallow back his pain. He knew he would have to face the family eventually. He couldn't hide out in his bedroom much longer as if he couldn't hear their excited voices. But he needed another moment to absorb the truth.

Destiny Fisher was going to marry Sean.

CHAPTER 1

Twelve years later...

"Wouldn't it be easier to just go to another bar?"

Destiny slammed her shot glass down on the table, shuddered as the tequila ran down her throat, and shook her head. "Nope. We were here first. We aren't leaving." She focused her attention on Bex first and then glanced around at her other three friends, Christa, Libby, and Shayla. They were all staring at her with narrowed eyes of concern.

"I don't think it matters who got here first, Des," Bex said in a gentle voice. The quietest of the group, Bex placed her hand on top of Destiny's and gave it an understanding squeeze. "What matters is that you're uncomfortable." Her words were nearly comical since typically Bex was the shy one, the uncomfortable one. She said it was because, with her brown hair, green eyes, and average height, she was so ordinary that no one ever noticed her.

Destiny shook her head again, a bit too hard. She grabbed the edge of the table to steady herself. "I'm not uncomfortable. It's fine. The Ugly Mug is big enough for the both of us." She glanced once more toward the growing group of men standing around three bar tables shoved together, giving high-fives and obviously celebrating.

He was there. His back was to her, but she would know him anywhere.

She wasn't the only one stealing glances at the group. Every red-blooded woman in the place was looking. Not surprising. After all, this was Killeen, Texas, and they were only a few miles from Fort Hood. On any given night, the place was packed with military men, some in civilian attire, some in uniform. Didn't matter what they were wearing because it was easy to spot them from their physique, haircuts, and often, tattoos.

Destiny jerked her gaze back to the surface of the table, noting there were still four full shot glasses. She'd ordered a round of tequila shots for herself and her friends the moment she'd spotted him.

Trent Dawkins. She hadn't seen him in about six months this time, but he looked just the same. Tall, broad, built. His muscles bulged under his white T-shirt. The shirt could stand to be at least a size larger, but maybe he liked it tight. It certainly attracted attention. The bottom half of his tattoo peeked out beneath a short sleeve. She'd seen it many times. As far as Destiny knew, that was the only tattoo he had. Unless he'd added some ink since she'd last seen his naked chest.

She groaned at the thought of that vision, shook her head again, and reached for another shot. If her friends weren't going to join her, she'd drink them herself. She tipped that one back and slammed the glass down on the table a bit harder than necessary.

"Des? Maybe you should slow down a bit," Libby suggested. "We could go back to the hotel. Hang out, just the five of us. It would be quieter, anyway. We could order pizza and watch an old movie."

Destiny smiled at the friend to her left. Libby tucked a thick lock of dark, wavy hair behind her ear and forced a smile. Her flawless dark skin, a result of her Guatemalan heritage, made all of them envious. She was currently holding Destiny's gaze without flinching.

Destiny pursed her lips and inhaled through her nose. After a few seconds, she released the breath through her mouth. "Nope. I'm good."

Shayla nudged Destiny playfully from her other side, her pin-straight, black hair swaying over both their shoulders. "He's probably not half as amazing as your mind has turned him into over the years, anyway. After all, you said you haven't had a full conversation with him in over ten years. Maybe he's an asshole. Maybe he's slept with a woman in every port."

"He's not in the *Navy*," Christa teased. She rolled her eyes at Shayla and giggled, the dimples on her pale cheeks showing. She was the lightest of the five of them. No. That was an understatement. Her skin was so pale that she burned just thinking about the sun. Her blond hair was natural and almost white, her eyes a pale blue.

"Every desert then," Shayla joked. "Whatever. That's not the point."

Destiny tipped back a third shot and tuned her friends out, her gaze wandering toward Trent's back again. She didn't believe it. There was no way he had turned into some womanizing dick. It wasn't in his blood. No matter what life had tossed at him, Destiny knew he would remain the same guy she'd known most of her life. Kind. Funny. Laughing. Light. The fun guy. Always saw the best in people. An extrovert.

God, she missed him.

She missed the way he'd teased her, even when they were in Kindergarten. She missed the way he said her name. He was the first person to give her the nickname *Des* long before anyone else started calling her that, and no one had ever said it quite the way he did. Like a long syllable. Softly spoken. Even when they were kids, he would hold her gaze as he whispered her name. More so in high school, up until she started dating his twin, Sean.

Destiny shuddered at the memory. Those days were long gone. In the past. Another lifetime.

Suddenly, as if he sensed someone staring at him, Trent turned around. His gaze quickly scanned the area until it landed on hers.

She should have glanced away before he caught her looking, but she couldn't. She was drawn to him like a magnet, unable to move or breathe as the clock ticked but time stood still. She wasn't sure how long they stared at each other, but finally, he smiled, whispered something to the guy next to him, and headed her direction.

"Shit." Destiny gripped the table again. The room was swaying a bit. She should not have done that many shots.

Her friends glanced back and forth between her and Trent, murmuring under their collective breaths. "Uh-oh," one of them whispered.

"This is not going to go well," Libby stated.

When Trent finally reached their booth, he seemed even larger than she remembered, looming over the five of them. Broader. More muscular. He probably was. Hell, he probably worked out ten hours a day.

"Des."

She shivered at the sound of his voice, the way he spoke her name just as he always had. Reverently. As if she were royalty or something. Her body responded to his tone also, her nipples stiffening, her pussy clenching.

This—this reaction to just her name from his lips—this was why she'd chosen to avoid him since after high school. He melted her resolve when he spoke to her. If she let him get to her, really corner her and force her to speak to him, she feared she would share all her secrets. Secrets she would take to the grave.

"I didn't know you were in town," he stated before he glanced at her friends. "Ladies." He nodded toward each of them.

"You must be Trent," Libby said. A second later, she gasped, and Destiny assumed Bex had kicked her under the table.

Trent smiled at her, obviously not unaware that it was extremely telling that this stranger knew who he was without introductions. "I am." He held out a hand. "And you are?"

"Libby," she breathed out, a bit starstruck. Not surprising. She had a thing for men in uniform. She sat up straighter, which did very little to make her four-foot eleven frame seem larger. "This is Christa, Bex, and Shayla," she continued, pointing around the table.

Trent nodded again at each of them.

"We work together," Christa stated.

"For the airline. Open Skies," Libby added.

Bex said nothing, but she was leaning forward slightly. No one was unaffected by Trent.

Trent shifted his gaze back to Destiny. "Do you have a few minutes? I'd love to catch up."

Destiny's heart raced. She'd love nothing more than to catch up with Trent. Hell, she would enjoy doing far more than that with him, but she wouldn't. She shouldn't. Just being near him was dangerous to her heart and her resolve. She opened her mouth to make an excuse, but Shayla quickly scooted from the booth and grabbed Destiny's arm to tug her across the seat. Before Destiny could wrap her head around this bad idea, she was standing—swaying really—in front of Trent.

He frowned slightly, but his eyes were still dancing as he took her arm to steady her. "I'll bring her back to you in one piece," he told her friends as he led her away from the security of her posse.

She glanced back, begging her friends with her eyes

to intervene. *Say something*. They waved and shooed her off. Great. Wonderful. Just what she needed.

Trent's hand slid down to grasp hers, and he wove through several people until they reached a corner. The noise level was lower in this spot, but Destiny's anxiety level was higher. *What does he want?*

This was not good.

CHAPTER 2

Trent was still stunned to have found Destiny here tonight. He hadn't seen her for months, and she hadn't spoken to him intentionally or looked him in the eye since high school. He wasn't stupid. He knew she'd ignored him for the last dozen years. He even understood why. But he was done with that shit. Right now.

This wasn't a decision he'd pondered often or even recently, but the second he saw her laughing and drinking with her friends, he made the spontaneous decision to face her eye to eye and force their weird awkwardness to take a hike.

He got it. Really, he did. She'd been in love with his brother, Sean, and mourned him. It probably hurt too bad for her to face Trent and pretend everything was fine. Hell, it hurt him too. Sean might have been her fiancé, but he was Trent's twin brother. They'd been close from the moment they were born. The pain of losing Sean was tremendous. The pain of losing his best friend at the same time had been more than he could bear.

Although that wasn't entirely true, he'd lost his best friend more than a year before he lost Sean. He'd lost Destiny when she started dating Sean and Trent hadn't been able to face her. The angst of watching her with his brother had been too much. So, it was entirely Trent's fault that he'd turned his back on her while they were still in high school.

But tonight, he'd look her straight in the eye.

He backed her into the corner, angled her so her fine ass was against the wall, and crowded her. *Damn, she's gorgeous*. Twelve years ago, she hadn't quite filled out. Now...she had more of a figure. She was still slim and lithe with long legs and not an ounce of fat on her, but she had boobs and curves.

Her tight curls that had been unruly when she was a kid were tamed into submission. He kinda missed the wild look but figured she found this to be more sophisticated. Her skin was a gorgeous honey tone that everyone envied. Her father had been African American or perhaps from the Caribbean while her mother was white, and she'd gotten perfect skin that made anyone glance twice. Including Trent.

The white, formfitting dress she wore had spaghetti straps and barely extended over her fantastic ass. The white wedge heels made her legs go on forever.

"How are you?" he asked, unable to pull his thoughts together and decide what he wanted to say.

"Good. Fine. You?" She tipped her head back and smiled at him, swaying slightly to one side.

He grabbed her shoulders to steady her. Yeah, she was drunk. He drew in a breath, catching her scent and nearly groaning. She still smelled like vanilla. Whatever body wash and lotion she'd used as a teenager was still her preference. "Living life." *Missing you.*

It was ridiculous that he still harbored feelings for her after all these years, but no matter how much time went by or how many women he dated, he still longed for what could have been if he'd played his cards differently.

She glanced down at his chest. "You look good. I think you get broader every time I see you." She patted his chest and then removed her hand as if he'd burned her. As if she were shocked that he was as solid as she suspected.

"I work out a lot," he explained lamely. "In between missions, I mean."

She leaned around him and then grabbed his arm when she had trouble righting herself again. "You have a lot of friends with you tonight."

He set a hand on her biceps to keep her from swaying. Did she often drink like this? "Yeah. My team and another. We've been on a few missions that caused us to cross paths lately."

"Where are you stationed now? Still in D.C.?"

He shook his head. "No. We just got transferred here to Fort Hood actually. I've hardly unpacked. My last mission was in Kazarus protecting my buddy's woman."

"Successful, I hope." She lifted a brow.

"Yes. Nori is Woof's high school sweetheart in fact. We're all relieved they're reconnected."

Destiny nodded and whispered, "That's so sweet."

He swallowed, wanting to kick himself. Life had not been as kind to Destiny. His brother had not returned to her. Obviously, it still hurt. As far as he knew, she'd never moved on. His mother kept up with her life through Destiny's grandmother, and she always made a point of telling Trent the unwanted details when he was in town.

He'd considered telling his mother to stop a long time ago but hadn't wanted her to know how much it hurt. How it would be easier if he didn't think about Destiny. How he'd loved her at least as much as Sean. Since not a single living soul ever knew that, he would carry his pain to the grave.

Trent was probably out of his mind for cornering her like this at all.

He'd told himself he wanted to end the awkwardness. But he knew that was a lie. He'd wanted to be close to her. Stand in her space. Inhale her scent. Touch her. Even if this was all he got for another five years, it was better than nothing. Better even than spending a whole night with a woman he barely knew.

He might regret the decision, however, judging by the memories flooding his system. When she rocked from one foot to the other in a way she always did when she was nervous, his chest tightened. She kept tucking her hair behind her ears, too. It wasn't as necessary today as it had been when they were kids, but she probably did it out of habit.

"How's your mom?" she asked, licking her lips.

"She's good. Dad's retired now, so he's driving her crazy with his projects around the house. I saw your grandmother yesterday in the yard. She looked well." This was why he needed to fix things between them. He would never be able to escape her since his parents lived next door to her grandmother. Neither party seemed inclined to move, and all three were healthy and happy.

"Yeah, she's got a lot of energy. I don't think she's going to slow down anytime soon. Even though she's my grandmother, she's hardly older than your parents."

He nodded. Stella Fisher had her own daughter at a young age. And Dina, Destiny's mother, had gotten pregnant at nineteen. When Dina disappeared and Destiny came to live with Stella, Destiny was five and Stella was only forty-three. The woman wasn't even seventy yet, and she still seemed fifty to Trent.

A waitress appeared next to them with a tray of colorful shots. "Can I interest either of you in a shot?"

Destiny immediately grabbed a clear one. "Yes. Thank you." She pointed toward her table. "Can you add it to my bill?"

"Of course. Enjoy." The woman wandered away.

Trent watched as Destiny tipped her head back and downed the liquid. Her neck elongated, making him wish he could slide his fingers up and cup her face. He'd never get to do something like that in this lifetime, but he could dream.

When she righted herself, she swayed again.

"How many of those have you had?"

She shrugged. "Lost count."

"Special occasion? I know it's not your birthday." He had that memorized for life, too.

"Nope."

"Do you always drink like this?" Maybe she had a problem. Maybe she hadn't been able to move on at all after Sean died. Trent hated that for her.

"Nope." She lifted her hand to shove at his chest. "Are you done interrogating me? I should get back to my friends."

He grabbed her forearms when it seemed she might fall into him, though half of him thought he should have simply let her collide with his chest. At least he would have gotten a chance to find out what she would feel like against his body.

"I'd rather you look me in the eye and talk to me for a few minutes. We've been dancing around each other awkwardly for twelve years. I miss our friendship. I know my brother's death was hard on you. It was hard on me, too. I miss him every day. Can't we talk about it instead of ignoring it?" He had no idea why he was pushing her. This was probably a bad idea, especially since she'd done several shots.

She stiffened, grabbed his shirt, and tipped her head back to look him in the eye. "No, we can't fucking talk about it." She shook her head, which made her tilt to one side again.

He grabbed her waist and held her upright. She was drunk, but her tone shocked him. "Why not?"

She glared at him. "Are you really that dense?"

Apparently, but he didn't get a chance to respond

because she kept talking. Her words came out so fast that he could only stare at her with his mouth hanging open.

"Don't you get it? I can't be around you." She shook her head hard. "Ever. Not ever again. It hurts to even look at you." Her eyes brimmed with tears.

Trent couldn't breathe. He'd been right. She missed his brother so much that she couldn't face Trent.

"I was in love with you, Trent. I was in love with you, and you never knew it. I fucked up my entire life when I agreed to marry your brother. I never should have gone out with him on that first fucking date. It was you I wanted." Her voice was cracking and loud, but the bar was too noisy for anyone to hear her.

Trent sucked in a sharp breath. He couldn't process her words. His brain wouldn't keep up.

She didn't stop talking, her words spilling out with alarming clarity as if she were no longer under the influence of several shots. "Sean was so nice and so sweet and I knew how much he liked me. So, I said yes when he first asked me out. And I kept saying yes for months. And we kept dating. And you stopped talking to me and hardly looked at me. And everything changed between us. And I missed you so much it hurt. And I wanted you to see me. And you didn't. And then your brother asked me to marry him before he left for boot camp, and I was stupid and said *yes* because I knew it was expected of me.

"Your mom was so in love with the idea of me marrying Sean that she never stopped grinning. I think she had china patterns picked out before he asked me.

And you didn't want me. So, I thought I should just do it. But it hurt. It ruined everything. The three of us were inseparable for thirteen years and then boom. It was over. And I had been feeling differently about you for over a year by then. And you didn't feel the same. And I didn't know what to do. And I made bad choices. And I have to live with them."

Trent swallowed hard. *My God. Oh my God.*

Her small fingers fisted in his T-shirt and she shook him. Tears gleamed at the corners of her eyes. Her voice was hoarse and filled with emotion. "And now the entire damn town feels sorry for me. For the poor girl whose heart was broken when her high school sweetheart went off to war and was killed before we made it to the altar." She gave a sardonic laugh and continued. "If they only knew how many other things we didn't do before he died."

Fuck.

"So, no. We can't be friends, Trent. Not ever. And I can't look you in the eye because frankly, I'm still half in love with you. And you don't feel the same, and it hurts so badly that I can't breathe when we're in the same room. So, please. Let me go on with my stupid miserable life. If you see me again, turn the other way." Those last words came out on a sob, the tears finally falling.

She sagged against him now, her forehead on his chest.

He wrapped his arms around her and held her tighter than he'd ever held another human in his life.

Fuck me. He tried to process everything she'd just said, but it wasn't possible. He needed hours. Days.

Destiny hiccupped and then groaned, shoving him back. "I'm gonna puke." She turned and rushed toward the restrooms.

Trent followed her, staying right on her heels as she passed the line of people waiting, shoved the next person out of the way as someone left one of the three unisex bathrooms, and lunged for the toilet, reaching it just in time.

Trent grabbed her hair and held it back, waiting while she emptied the contents of her stomach. It took a while, which didn't surprise him considering how much she probably drank.

"Is she okay?"

Trent turned to find one of her friends squeezing into the small room. The door was standing wide open and several people waiting in line had backed up.

"How much did she have before I approached?" Trent asked the blonde.

"Several shots." She grabbed a handful of paper towels, dipped them under the faucet, and handed them to Trent as if he were in charge of this disaster. And she was not wrong. He was. In a perfect world, he would be in charge of everything that related to Destiny for the rest of his life.

He was still processing everything she'd told him, but he knew one thing for sure—she was not alone. And he needed to make sure she got that through her head.

He crouched beside her and wiped her face with the

wet paper towels. She moaned as she slowly stood and met his gaze for a moment. "Shit," she muttered.

The blonde spoke again. He tried to remember what her name was. Christa maybe. He hadn't been paying close attention to all their names when they'd been introduced. "We have a hotel room. I'll tell the girls we need to leave."

He shook his head. "No. You stay. Enjoy yourselves. I'll take her to my place. Let her sleep it off."

Christa held his gaze, chewing on her bottom lip, considering his words. "I don't think she would like that."

He chuckled as Destiny leaned into him, grabbing his waist to remain upright. "I'm certain you're right, but it's the right thing to do. And we need to talk. Des and I. It would seem we should have done so years ago. We've both been living in separate Mansions of Misery." He had little doubt her posse was well aware of how Destiny felt about him, especially judging by the look of hesitation on her friend's face. "Don't worry. I won't touch her. I'll fill her with ibuprofen and water and put her to bed. I'm not an asshole."

Christa nodded. "Okay. You're sure?"

"Positive." For once in his life, he was certain of something when it came to Destiny.

Christa backed out of the small bathroom.

Trent followed, holding Destiny to his side. He led her back to the table and accepted the purse one of her other friends held out. They were all staring at him with hope in their eyes. *Yes, they knew*. Apparently, he was the only fool in the vicinity who had not known Destiny was into him.

When he turned around, he was faced with several of his team members. He'd practically forgotten who he'd come with. Thank God he'd driven himself.

"Zip?" Merlin looked concerned as he addressed Trent by his nickname. He was the oldest of their team, but only by a year. Nevertheless, they all looked to him as their unofficial leader.

"Rescuing damsels in distress?" Woof asked in a teasing voice.

"Something like that," he murmured.

"Where are you going?" Jangles asked, his blue eyes filled with concern. Trent was a little surprised he was even standing with the other guys instead of flirting with the bartender, Hope. Seemed like that was all he did lately when they came to the Ugly Mug.

"My apartment. She needs to sleep this off."

Duff stepped to her other side and helped Trent make his way toward the door. "Know her?"

"Yes. Since we were small kids." Trent supported her as best he could, but she staggered all the way to the door. Totally out of it.

"Ah, okay." Duff opened the door and held it. "Careful. Text if you need anything." That handful of words was the most Duff had said all night.

"Will do. Tell the guys I said goodbye." He'd hardly had a chance to speak to most of them. Lefty disappeared the second Kinley showed up, and the rest of his team had spent the next fifteen minutes high-fiving each other. Trent would see them all frequently now that his team was in Fort Hood. Within no time, they would be reacquainted.

Right now, he needed to focus on Destiny. Until he had her tucked into bed, he wouldn't let himself ponder everything she had just revealed. He couldn't. If he did, he would drive off the road.

CHAPTER 3

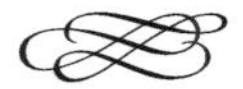

Destiny moaned as she turned onto her side and drew her arm over her eyes. Why was her bedroom so bright? She never left the blinds open when she went to bed.

Her head pounded as she tried to recall if she'd had a bit too much to drink last night. Her memory started coming back. She'd gone out with the girls last night. They were in Killeen for the weekend. They had a hotel room. She'd done some tequila shots...

She inhaled slowly. The masculine scent that assaulted her nose, however familiar, did not belong on her pillow. She froze.

Please tell me I didn't hook up with a stranger. She sniffed the pillow again. *Or worse...*

Trent.

Oh shit.

Right. She'd run into Trent.

Wait...

Oh no. *Oh no oh no oh no.* She bolted to sitting, gasping for oxygen. As she glanced around, she recognized nothing, but she knew exactly where she was. She could smell Trent everywhere. This was his bedroom.

She groaned out loud before she could stop herself and then jerked her gaze toward the door, fearing he might have heard her. "Shit," she muttered as she swung her legs over the side of the bed. There was a glass of water and two pills on the bedside table. Of course there was. Trent always thought of everything.

She shook that thought from her mind. It wasn't true. At least it hadn't been when they were younger. Sean thought of everything. He was meticulous and serious and planned every detail. Trent was more laid back. He preferred to wing it.

But Sean wasn't here. Trent was. And he'd left her ibuprofen.

Destiny quickly swallowed the pills and downed the water, feeling much better after getting the fluids in her. She quietly eased herself up until she stood on slightly shaky legs, taking note of the fact that she was still wearing her dress and her shoes were next to the bed.

As she padded gingerly toward the attached bathroom, she cringed. Had she slept with Trent? That would be a disaster. She looked back over her shoulder and noticed the other side of his bed didn't look like it had been slept in. That was a good sign. Wasn't it?

She used the toilet and then winced as she met her gaze in the mirror. Her hair was a curly mess sticking out all over. Her mascara was smudged. Her cheeks looked gaunt. She quickly washed her face, clearing the makeup away as best she could with splashes of water, and then used the new toothbrush she found on the counter.

Already she felt better, but she still had to face Trent. Taking a deep breath, she padded from the room and into the hallway, discovering that to her immediate right was a living room and kitchen area. Trent was sitting on the couch staring at his phone, but he lifted his gaze when she entered.

For a moment they stared at each other, and then he smiled slightly and cleared his throat. "How do you feel?"

She tipped her face toward the floor and rubbed the bridge of her nose with two fingers. "Like I drank too much and said some things." *Shit. I said a lot of things, didn't I?* She searched her brain, trying to remember everything she'd blurted out. It was hazy, but she knew it was bad.

"You did indeed drink too much, but lucky for you, vomiting at the bar and then twice when we got back here probably saved you from a horrific hangover." He rose to his feet. "As for saying some things, you definitely did."

For a moment, she thought he was going to approach her, but instead, he headed for the kitchen. "I'll pour you some juice and make you some breakfast. Come. Sit at the table." He pointed to his small kitchen table next to the passthrough galley kitchen.

Destiny didn't move for a moment. She couldn't imagine what she was going to say. How was he so calm? Her words from last night flooded in.

Shit. Shit shit shit. "Maybe it would be best if I called an Uber and left."

He tilted his head to one side and gazed at her. "Not a chance. Sit," he demanded again.

She blew out a breath and headed toward the table, wishing there was a crack in the universe that might swallow her whole. That would be too easy though. As she took a seat, Trent set a tall glass of orange juice in front of her without another word. He turned back around to put bacon in the heating pan. The sizzle filled the room before the scent. Her stomach growled.

Her mortification crept back in as soon as she finished half the juice. "Trent… Listen."

He turned around, shaking his head. "Nope. Not my turn to listen. Let me finish cooking so you can get some food in you, and then *you* can listen. How about that?" His words were clipped. His tone was off. His usual easy-going demeanor was not present.

Shit.

All Destiny could do was wait and watch as he worked. It was impossible not to notice how amazing his body still was. Actually, it was even better than she remembered. He was wearing gray Army sweats and a navy Army T-shirt that hugged his chest and stretched tight across his back. His feet were bare. His hair was wet, she noted. Which meant he'd taken a shower before she got up. *How the hell did I sleep through that?*

"I left you a towel in the bathroom if you want to shower," he commented as he flipped the bacon. "You can borrow one of my T-shirts if you don't want to put your dress back on."

Her heart was beating too fast. No way was she going to shower at Trent Dawkins' apartment. *Nope. Horrible idea.* Almost as bad as sitting here waiting to hear what he was going to say to her.

Was he pissed that she had so badly defiled his brother's memory by admitting she'd been in love with Trent instead? She rubbed her temples, letting her eyes slide closed. *How could I be so stupid?*

After a few minutes of silence, Trent slid a plate in front of her and then sat in the chair adjacent to hers with a steaming cup of coffee. "Eat. You'll feel better."

She lifted her gaze. "Seriously?" Did he think food would make her feel better? Even though her stomach was in a tight ball, part of her was afraid that was from nerves instead of hunger. She might actually vomit again if she ate.

Trent wrapped both hands loosely around his mug and lifted his gaze to meet hers. His voice was calm and even when he spoke. "Destiny, I slept like shit. I spent the entire night trying to absorb everything you said to me and come up with a response. I know you were drunk when you said all that stuff, but I also know it was all true. You took a risk. Now, you owe me a chance to respond. And I'm going to do so after you eat." He let go of the mug with one hand and slid it across the table to wrap his fingers around one of her hands and squeeze gently. "You're shaking. You need food. Eat," he repeated. "And then we'll talk."

She blew out a breath and nodded. What choice did she have? He was right. She'd made a complete fool out of herself, and now she needed to face the consequences. "Okay, but can I just say that I'm sorry. I know what I said was out of line. I should have taken those thoughts to the grave with me. I had no business blurting out my deepest secrets to you like that. You have every right to be mad at me. I dishonored Sean's memory then, and I did so again last night. I'm truly sorry."

Trent closed his eyes and breathed in and out deeply. "Destiny..."

"Yes?"

"Eat." He pointed at her food and stood. "Do you want coffee?" he said as he padded back into the kitchen.

"Yes. Thank you," she murmured.

"You still take it with cream and sugar?"

"Please." He remembered how she took her coffee. That fact alone reached into her soul and made her sigh.

Her hands trembled as she picked up her fork, but she somehow managed to take a bite and then another. With each bite, she grew hungrier, and soon enough she had polished off everything.

Trent slid a mug of coffee—made exactly how she liked it—in front of her. He set a hand on her shoulder and gave a gentle squeeze. "Feel better?"

"Yes. Thank you."

"How about we move to the sofa?"

She lifted the coffee, took a fortifying sip, and followed him across the room as if she were heading to the guillotine. She deserved to feel this way—her heart clenched and her pulse raced too fast. She was a complete idiot. And whatever he said to reprimand her she deserved.

She considered insisting that he keep his thoughts to himself and let her leave, but that would be selfish and a cop-out. She'd dug this hole. Now she needed to lie in it.

Trent sat in the sofa corner and then reached for her coffee and set it on the end table. Before she could decide where to sit exactly, he grabbed her hand and pulled her down next to him, practically on top of him, actually. He wrapped her in his arms and hauled her against his chest, his fingers sliding into her hair and rubbing her back.

She tried to relax into his comforting touch, but confusion warred inside her. *Why is he being so nice? He should be furious*. She trembled against him.

"Shhh," he whispered against her head. "Take a breath. It's going to be okay."

She jerked her face back to look up at him. "It's never going to be okay. I have to live with my stupidity for the rest of my life. I'm mortified beyond belief. How can you even say that?"

He smiled as his hand slid around and he stroked her cheek. "Because even though you took me by surprise and shocked the hell out of me, I had the entire night to think about what you said while you were snoring off your drunken stupor."

She drew her brows together. "I don't snore."

"Ha." His smile grew and his eyes twinkled. "Whatever. I'll record you next time."

Next time? She flinched.

"Yeah, you heard me." He glanced down at her lips and trailed his thumb along the seam. "Des." He lifted his eyes slowly. "I can't tell you how happy I am that you got drunk last night and spilled your guts. If you hadn't, we may have gone our entire lives not knowing how the other felt."

"What?" She stiffened, confused.

He nodded. "I was a coward back then, and I've been a coward ever since. I had no idea you felt that way about me, or I would have told you I felt the same way."

She jerked in his arms, and she was pretty sure her heart stopped. "What?" she repeated.

He nodded, a slight smile on his lips. "It killed me when you started dating Sean. Ripped a hole in me that never fully healed. I drank enough to pass out the night you got engaged. Stole a bottle of vodka from my father's liquor cabinet."

She leaned back a few more inches, shaking her head, unable to believe his words. "You stopped talking to me and never met my gaze after my first date with Sean. The way you were acting…at the time, I thought you didn't like me, didn't care about me anymore. I thought I might die the next time I saw you and you ignored me. My life crumbled slowly away while day after day I held your brother's hand and tried to convince myself I was doing the right thing."

Trent's thumb stroked her cheek again. "I was so confused, and it was all so complicated. And I thought you were in love with him, so I forced myself to give you space. Both of you. But I couldn't continue to pretend everything was fine, so I backed off. It hurt too badly to hang out with you guys anymore."

She held his gaze, but her heart was beating out of her chest. Her mind spun.

"I'm so sorry," he continued. "For so many things. But mostly because I was such a coward that I let you spend twelve years thinking I didn't care about you, when all that time, I never once stopped thinking about you and what might have been."

Trent. Her Trent. He was right here. Holding her. Looking her in the eye the way she'd dreamed of for so long. She'd dated dozens of guys over the years, but she'd never been able to let herself go with anyone and broke up with them within weeks. All because she never got Trent out of her mind.

By now, she wasn't even sure who he was anymore. It was possible she wouldn't even like the man he'd turned out to be. Her imagination had embellished him over the years, turning him into some sort of god. Perhaps he was actually a dick.

Trent took a deep breath. "Remember when we were ten and I slipped into that ravine and cut my thigh on that rusty pipe?"

She nodded. She hadn't been there. Only Sean had been there. And thank God, because he'd saved his brother's life. But she'd heard the story over and over. Everyone had.

"Yes. Of course."

"My life changed that day."

"You almost died."

"Yes. But I didn't. I was being stupid. Taking risks.

Sean didn't want me to climb down that embankment. He kept urging me to stop. Always the serious one. But I was laughing and joking and maybe even taunting him. And then I slipped and fell several feet. I saw the pipe before I hit it, but I couldn't stop it from impaling my thigh and ripping a ten-inch hole in my leg."

Destiny nodded again. She'd heard all this dozens of times. Trent had spent two days in the hospital. He'd needed a blood transfusion and over a hundred stitches, some inside and some outside.

"Sean saved my life. He was so calm even under pressure. He quickly eased down the embankment and tied his shirt around my leg. He scrambled back up that hill and screamed like hell at every passing car until someone stopped. At some point, I passed out, but he didn't give up. He saved me."

"I know all that, Trent," she responded soothingly. It obviously still stuck out in Trent's mind.

"I made myself a promise that I would be the best brother in the world that day, and I kept it."

Destiny flinched. *What is he saying?*

"When Sean came to me and told me he was going to ask you out on a real date, I died a little inside. I'd been looking at you as far more than the girl next door for years. The only reason I hadn't made a move was because I was afraid it would ruin our friendship if you turned me down."

"But Sean beat you to it," she whispered.

"Yes. And I stepped back. I owed him. I owed him everything. There was no way in the world I would have told him that I wanted you. It would've killed him.

At the time, he was so excited, and I'd never seen him that happy. He wasn't exactly a demonstrative guy."

She smiled wanly. "I remember."

"And then he asked you out, and you said yes, and I died a little more. And every day, a piece of me chipped off while you two became an item. You walked through the hallways at school holding hands and whispering and shit, and I turned around and went the other way every chance I got."

"I'm so sorry, Trent." Her throat clogged and tears formed in her eyes at the thought of everything the two of them had withheld. Nevertheless, she had been engaged to his brother, and she had to carry that burden with her now.

Trent swallowed. "Me, too. So sorry. And the worst part is that if I had to do it all over again, I would change nothing. I would never have crossed Sean like that. Never. I feel guilty even voicing it today, and he's been gone almost twelve years."

"Me, too," she whispered. "It's like survivor's guilt. It's lodged inside me. It's why I left town and moved to Dallas and became a flight attendant. I couldn't stand to walk around Killeen any longer. Everyone in town knew who I was and that my fiancé had died in battle. I felt horrible because a part of me was not nearly as sad as I was supposed to be." Destiny grabbed Trent's forearms and squeezed them. "Don't get me wrong. I loved Sean dearly. But I loved him like a brother. And I ached for his loss, same as everyone else, but not the way I should have. Not the way a girlfriend would. I wasn't *in* love with him."

Trent rubbed her back again. "I get it now."

"Do you? Because I'm not sure *I* do. It's confusing and it tears me apart every time I think about it. Your mother loved me like I was her own daughter. She was so excited when we got engaged that I thought she might float."

Destiny smiled faintly. "Everyone thought we were the cutest couple in the world. Some people stopped whispering about the fact that I'm biracial, even called out those who didn't. It felt like almost everyone was in love with the idea of us, except me."

She shook her head. "I don't know why I said *yes,* but maybe that was part of it, feeling like maybe I belonged for once. It was stupid. I was too young and naïve, and I kept telling myself it would be okay. That he was a great guy. That I would grow to love him in time. Inside, I was dying and alone. I never told anyone until years later."

"But your girlfriends know, right? The ones from last night?"

"Yeah. Eventually, I was busting with the weight of the secret, and I told them one night a few years ago. They've pressured me to confront you ever since. I never had the guts."

One side of his mouth tipped up. "Tequila speaks."

"I guess so."

He held her gaze for a long time and then licked his lips. "Now what do we do?"

"Nothing." She shook her head, her heart aching all over again. She wiggled free of his grasp before she could lose her willpower. Letting him touch her and hold her had been a mistake. She pushed to standing and took a step back.

Trent looked up at her, eyes wide, shock registering. "Why would we do that?"

"Because people would be horrified if I dated you."

"It's been twelve years, Des. I don't think you need to continue mourning my brother."

She took another step back, digging her heels in. She had to. "Can you imagine how your parents would feel? Especially your mom?" Destiny shuddered at the visual of William's and Nancy's faces if they ever found out about this. Nancy's eyes would pop out of her head, and she'd probably never speak to Destiny again, or her grandmother. Dating his brother would put salt in a wound that never healed. Not for Nancy or William.

"Des..." Trent stood and took a step closer. "I think you're overreacting."

She shook her head vehemently. "Nope. And we'll never know because I don't ever want to face your mother and break her heart like that."

Trent kept coming toward her. "Des, my mother loves you to pieces."

"Yep. I know she does. So, let's not ruin it by telling her what a horrible person I was and still am."

"You're not a horrible person, Des. You're human. I made just as many mistakes as you did. I don't think my parents would be upset about this. In fact, they might even be elated."

Destiny ran out of space, her back hitting the wall. She'd never in twelve years pictured a scenario like this. She'd been convinced that Trent saw her as an annoying woman who preferred his serious brother over his extroverted, fun-loving self. It was impossible to process the conversation they'd just had, but no matter what, no one would understand if she switched brothers. It would taint the memory of her dead fiancé.

Trent kept advancing. When he reached her, he flattened his palms on the wall on either side of her head, his face coming in close even though no part of him touched her. "We both spent twelve years totally misunderstanding each other. I won't waste another day without spending time with you. Maybe we've both changed too much to still have feelings for each other, but what if we haven't? I want to know. Don't you?"

Her breath hitched.

"I seriously doubt a single person in this town is going to give one shit if we get together. But even if they strung me up by my heels and taped a scarlet A on my shirt, I would still prefer to give this a chance. To hell with all of them."

Destiny's heart leaped. Butterflies fluttered in her stomach. She found it impossible to believe this was happening. An hour ago, when she'd awakened in Trent's bed, she'd dreaded this confrontation more than getting a tooth extracted. And now... How had things taken such a sharp turn?

"I'm going to kiss you now with every ounce of passion I've felt for over a decade." He hesitated only long enough to read her acceptance in her gaze, and then his lips descended.

Destiny grabbed his T-shirt and yanked him against her the moment his mouth met hers. His kiss was filled with frantic desperation, the same desperation she felt. Tongues tangled and moans filled the room, coming from both of them.

Trent tasted like coffee and heaven. His hands cupped her face and angled her head exactly where he wanted it.

She slid her palms to his ass and gripped him with the tips of her fingers. Her brain was mush. No one had ever kissed her like this before. Not with this much passion. She never wanted it to end. She would be content to spend the rest of her life right here in Trent's living room in a lip lock. He kissed so well that she didn't even need to know if they were compatible in any other way.

It was hard to say how long they might have continued kissing, but Trent's phone rang, interrupting them. Trent continued for another moment, his tongue running along the seam of her lips before he released her mouth and groaned. "Horrible timing."

"You should get that," she murmured, trying to catch her breath.

He gave no indication he intended to move for several long seconds, holding her gaze while the ringing stopped.

She knew him though. His life was not his own. He belonged to the Army. He didn't have the luxury of ignoring a phone call. When he was not on an assignment, his job at Fort Hood was to keep in shape and wait for the next call.

"I will. In a minute. But first, let me say that you just rocked my world and tipped it upside down. If you're thinking of continuing to argue that we shouldn't explore this thing between us, don't. I'm not buying it. We are so totally going to spend every possible moment together, figuring this out and getting to know each other all over again. Got it?"

She nodded, smiling a little. "I can't argue your point, but I can insist we keep this to ourselves. I'm not facing your mom and risking her thinking ill of me while we take this risk. If it doesn't work out, then she never needs to know it happened."

He hesitated for several seconds and then sighed. "Okay. Not forever, mind you. I'm feeling impatient. But for now."

"This is going to get complicated."

He nodded in agreement. "It is."

"My grandmother's going to be disappointed, too."

"Why?" He furrowed his brow. "She's never been judgmental, Des."

She blew out a breath. "I know you never fully understood what it was like for me to grow up in this town, half white, half black. It was never easy."

"Des, you know color didn't matter like that when my parents looked at you. Not for a second. And I'm not buying that it mattered to your grandmother, either."

"You're right, and your mother in particular made my childhood better than I could have ever hoped. She babysat me when Grandma had to work. She hugged me and told me she loved me. *Me*. A girl with no mother of her own. It meant the world to me. But to the rest of the town, I was never good enough. I'm not black enough for the black folks, nor am I white enough for the white folks.

"I was only about seven years old when Grandma gave me a serious lecture about how to face the struggles in my life. She told me the best way for me to be accepted by the rest of the town was to be a model citizen in all things. Never give anyone a reason to judge me. I think I did a pretty good job, but I walked a fine line. Even though a lot of people were supportive, I heard the rumors when Sean and I got engaged. I know some people had decided they could tolerate me living here, but marrying a white guy was crossing the line."

Trent sucked in a sharp breath. "Des, I had no idea you experienced that. But I should've."

She shrugged. "I didn't tell you, or anyone for that matter. No one other than my grandmother, that is. But don't you see? Switching brothers even after all these years would cause rampant rumors. Just think of what they'd say."

"You're strong. Ignore them. Why do you care what other people think?" He stroked her cheeks with his thumbs.

"I can't afford to think that way, to ignore them. I'm not the only one I'm worried about, Trent. You don't deserve the kind of harassment you'll get if people find out we're together. You haven't lived with it your whole life, so you don't get it."

He shook his head. "I don't give a single shit what the rest of the town thinks, Des."

"You say that now..."

"I mean it. Nothing could possibly make me turn away from you."

"Even if that weren't an issue, there are about a dozen other factors in our way. I live in Dallas. I work weird shifts and I'm sometimes gone for days. You just got to town, and your job means that you have to be prepared to drop everything at a moment's notice." She glanced toward where she thought the ringing had come. "That call might even now mean you're walking out the door and gone six months."

His eyes closed and he set his forehead against hers.

She'd only been stating the facts. She also acknowledged that there was no way she could avoid exploring what a relationship with him might look like. Maybe if they went on a date or something, they would realize they didn't even have that much in common anymore. It had been a long time. Both of them were basing their feelings on an inflated memory.

For a moment, she considered telling him she didn't want to see him again. It was too hard. Too complicated. It would hurt too badly when it fell apart. It would also hurt too badly if he was killed on a mission. That much she knew firsthand. Even though she hadn't been in love with Sean, she had loved him dearly, and she'd missed him terribly after he died. If anything ever happened to Trent…

But then the moment passed and she realized she would move hell and high water to spend even an hour with him halfway between Dallas and Killeen once every month if that was what it took.

Destiny decided maybe it would be better to throw

everything into the ring and see what happened. Maybe he would agree to spend some time with her without telling anyone. That way, if they realized they didn't have the spark they were imagining, no harm would be done.

His parents didn't need to know. Nor did the town. Or even her grandmother. They could meet in secret and keep it to themselves.

It didn't matter that logistically their lives were complicated. As long as he agreed to keep their relationship private, she was all-in. "Get the phone, Trent."

As if he hadn't been quick enough, a knock sounded at the door two seconds later.

Trent still held her gaze. "Fuck."

She ran her hands up and down his back. "It's okay. We waited a dozen years to say the things we blurted out this morning and last night. My heart is already lighter just knowing you'll be thinking about me."

"Every hour of every day."

"Get the door."

A voice called from outside. "Zip? Dude. What the hell?" More knocking.

Trent released her and backed up, still staring at her as he did so. It was a wonder he didn't fall over something. Finally, he spun around and rushed the last few feet, yanking the door open. "I'm here."

A man Destiny thought she remembered from the night before stepped inside. She hadn't quite connected him with Trent's buddies because he'd made a beeline for the bar when he came in. He was blond with blue eyes that were narrowed in a serious expression. When he caught Destiny out of his peripheral vision, he jerked his gaze to her and stopped moving.

Trent shut the door. "Destiny, this is Beau Talbot. We all call him Jangles."

"Sorry, ma'am. I didn't realize you were here. I should have remembered from last night."

"It's okay," she responded in a soft voice. She stood plastered to the wall. Her position had to look awkward.

Jangles shifted his gaze to Trent. "Sorry, Zip. We gotta go. Now."

Trent nodded. "Give me five minutes." He raced from the room, heading for his bedroom, pausing long enough to cup her face and mouth, *I'm sorry.*

When he was gone, she looked at Jangles. "Why do you call him Zip?"

"Because that gnarly scar on his thigh looks like a zipper from the way they stitched him up. We all decided it was the perfect nickname the first week we met."

She smiled. "Makes sense. It does look like a zipper. I never thought about it."

"You've known him a long time, right?"

"Yes. I moved in next door to his family when I was five."

"Right. You're Destiny. I remember you. You were, uh…" He stopped talking.

Destiny was going to have to get used to this if she intended to stick her feet in the sandbox. They might be able to keep their relationship mum from his parents and the community, but his team would know everything. They probably already did know more than she could imagine. And hell, her girlfriends were also well aware of him. "Yes. I was engaged to his twin brother."

Jangles nodded. "You should go talk to Zip while he packs. We don't have much time."

She liked Jangles immediately, and took his advice, spinning around to find Trent. Her heart was racing again, this time with nervous energy. She'd known he would leave eventually, but she hadn't expected it to be this soon. She rushed to his bedroom, feeling awkward.

He was already dressed and tugging his duffel closed. He reached for her and hauled her against him, giving her his full attention. "This sucks."

"Yeah."

"Take your time here. Shower. Whatever you need to do. I'll have Hatch come get you and take you back to your friends. His real name is Jason Nixon."

"Don't worry. I can have one of my girls come get me."

"You're sure?" His brow furrowed.

"Yes. I need to go see my grandmother this morning anyway and then we have to drive back to Dallas. I work tonight."

He nodded, swallowing. "Don't you dare fucking back out of this on me. The second I'm back in town, I'm heading to Dallas. I'll take a few days off if I can. I can't say how long I'll be gone."

The last thing she wanted was for him to worry about her ghosting him. It wasn't going to happen.

She'd given him her word. "I understand your job better than most, Trent. I'll be waiting. You just stay safe."

His eyes slid closed and he pulled her closer, kissing her lips quickly. "Thank you." He released her just as fast, hoisted his duffel, and heaved it onto his shoulder. As he left the room, he grabbed the door frame and looked back. "Spare key is in the right kitchen drawer. Take it. Use this place any time you want. If you're in town, stay here."

"Okay." She couldn't say more. Too much emotion welled up inside her.

Between one blink and the next, he was gone. She flinched as the door closed, leaving her in silence, a whirlwind of noise swirling around in her head nonetheless.

What the hell just happened?

CHAPTER 4

Two weeks later…

Trent sat in his black Corvette in front of Destiny's condo, staring at the front door but not moving. He'd arrived in Killeen two days ago after his mission wrapped up, but he'd needed time to debrief and deal with the possible fallout from the mission.

For the first time in his career, he was concerned about retribution. His entire team was worried about him. He'd been exposed during the mission, his mask yanked off in an altercation with the enemy. They knew who he was. One of the downsides of advancement in facial recognition. It was unlikely he would get blowback from the event, but everyone was on edge anyway. Watching. Assessing. Monitoring.

Nevertheless, Trent had the weekend off. And thank fuck, so did Destiny. He wanted to spend the next two days reacquainting himself with the girl he'd fallen for as a teenager. At the same time, he was completely dumbfounded at the thought of seeing her again. Their conversation two weeks ago in his apartment had been rushed and abruptly cut off. He'd thought about her every day since that morning, but until last night, he hadn't been able to contact her.

He'd also been too tongue-tied to call, so he'd sent her a text and then been relieved to find out she was currently in Seattle, but she would be back Friday afternoon.

Trent figured he'd beaten her to her condo, so he was still sitting in his car, staring at her door, fidgeting in his seat. He feared this was about to be the most awkward first date in the history of first dates. He'd never gone out with a woman *after* dumping his heart at her feet, and he doubted she'd ever done so either.

Hell, it seemed like neither of them had really had any serious relationships at all, considering they'd both been harboring feelings for each other extending back to high school.

The hardest part about coming to Dallas for the weekend had been explaining himself to his mom. So far, since moving to Killeen, he'd seen his parents a sum total of two times for about five minutes, so his mother definitely didn't understand what on earth he needed to do for the weekend that was more important than coming over to the house for a longer visit. And Trent wasn't about to tell her a single detail. Destiny thought it was important, and he sort of understood. After all, she was partially right about his mom. If they told her anything, she would get her hopes up. There was no guarantee that this thing they were exploring would end with them together. No sense giving his mother false hope.

Destiny had also made it clear that she didn't want them to be a public item. She was too embarrassed to face his parents. Trent had argued with her at the time that his parents might be shocked, but they would not be judgmental. He couldn't visualize any world in which his mom would think it was wrong for Trent to be dating Destiny. She'd probably be thrilled. Arguably *too* thrilled. He had to concede that point.

In moments of downtime during the past two weeks, Trent had warred with himself about confronting Destiny and nipping this secretiveness in the bud. But now he had a new problem. His last mission had been in Kazarus. The head of the Kazarus Freedom Army had Trent's identity, and the man was furious. Trent needed to lie low for a while.

The last thing he wanted was for Onur Demir to scope out anyone important in Trent's life and possibly come after Destiny or even his parents. So, he would use her demand to keep their relationship quiet to his advantage and play along. That would limit his contact with his mom and dad, and keep Destiny hidden.

He glanced at his watch. It was five o'clock. She said she would be home by five thirty as long as the flight wasn't delayed. He reached across to the passenger seat and tugged a worn envelope from the side pocket of his duffel. The edges were frayed and yellowing. He'd read the pages inside more times than he could count over the years. He'd never shared the letter with a living soul.

He didn't plan to today, either. Perhaps one day he would need to.

The letter was from Sean, and every time Trent held the pages, he choked up. His brother. The person with whom he'd shared a womb and had rarely separated from for eighteen years. The person he owed his life to. His best friend in the world.

Sean had written Trent this letter three days before he was killed in action. It had arrived a week after his death and left Trent shattered beyond belief. It still did every time he opened it. Trent had wondered for a decade if Sean had had some sort of premonition and thought he might be killed. Trent would never know.

Trent didn't open the letter now. It wasn't necessary. He knew what it said. He only pulled it out because it comforted him and gave him strength. It made him feel closer to his brother. In a way, forgiven for what he was about to do.

He closed his eyes and took several deep breaths, telling himself over and over that Sean would want Trent to be happy. He would definitely give his blessing if Trent pursued Destiny. He'd want Destiny to be happy, too.

Trent stuffed the letter back in his duffel. He was in no way prepared to share the letter with her. If by chance things between them didn't work out, she never needed to know it existed. Besides, he didn't want the letter's contents to influence her. Trent wanted to know in his heart that Destiny would choose him no matter what. If they managed to build something solid, there would come a time in the future when Trent would share the private correspondence, but not now, and certainly not until Trent was positive Destiny was fully into him on his own merit.

Trent nearly jumped out of his skin when a knock sounded against the window next to his head. He yanked his eyes open and turned to find Destiny standing beside his Corvette. She was biting her lower lip as she stepped back.

He opened the door to step out. *Damn, she looks good, even in her uniform.* The navy pencil skirt landed above her knees. She had on navy pumps, a white blouse with the Open Skies airline logo in the corner, and a matching navy jacket. She'd pulled her hair back in a loose bun.

He found himself nervous as a teenager as he faced her, shutting his car door without looking and then tucking the tips of his fingers in the back pockets of his jeans.

"You beat me here," she commented. "How long were you waiting?"

"Just a few minutes. I made good time."

She shrugged her purse up higher on her shoulder and nodded toward her apartment. "Come on. Let's go inside."

He reached for the roller bag she was pulling to take it from her, their fingers brushing against each other as he did so. That simple touch was enough to send a spark through his body. This thing between them was crazy. He prayed they could get over this awkward stage quickly and move on. He longed to hold her tightly in his arms.

Without a word, he followed her to her front door and waited while she unlocked it and pushed it open. When he stepped inside, he was surprised to find her roommate standing in the kitchen.

Destiny had told him she lived with one of her posse, Libby, last night in a text, but she hadn't said when or if Libby would be home. She had her own crazy flight schedule.

Part of Trent was disappointed. He'd wanted to be alone with Destiny. Another part of him felt relief. Having another person in the room might cut through some of the initial awkwardness.

"Hey," Libby said as she rounded the island to cross into the living room. She was holding a bottle of water, and she'd obviously been there a while because she was wearing black track shorts and a fuchsia tank top. Her thick wavy hair was pulled back in a ponytail. She smiled at Trent and held out a hand. "You made it. I'm Libby, if you forgot."

"Des told me." He shook her hand and then turned his attention to Destiny.

"Right, well, if you don't mind," Destiny said, "I'm just going to take a quick shower. I hate how I feel after I step off of a long flight."

"I understand. Go ahead."

"I'll keep him company," Libby stated.

Destiny sighed. "Okay, but don't grill him. He's a good guy. He doesn't require vetting."

Libby flattened a hand on her chest, eyes wide. "I don't grill your dates."

"Yes, you do. Every time." Destiny took her roller bag from Trent and pulled it toward the stairs.

He considered offering to carry it up for her but decided that was too forward. She could obviously handle it. She'd been doing so for years without any help. It wasn't in his nature to watch a woman haul luggage around, but it was even less in his nature to invite himself into her bedroom when he'd only been inside her apartment for two minutes.

"I'll be quick," she said as she disappeared up the stairs.

"Have a seat." Libby pointed at the beige sofa. "Can I get you anything to drink? Water? Beer? Soda?"

"Water would be great. Thanks." He turned around and surveyed the room while she headed for the refrigerator. It was a standard condo with beige carpeting and walls. There was an entertainment center across from the sofa, a matching love seat, end tables, and a coffee table. To bring some vibrancy to the room, the women had added jewel-toned throw pillows and colorful framed art.

"Here you go." Libby handed him a water bottle.

He lowered himself onto the sofa as she took a spot on the love seat and curled her legs under her. The woman was less than five feet tall, but he could sense already she had enough personality to make up for whatever she lacked in height. Her eyes danced with mischief. "Destiny says you've been on a mission. That's so cool. You must see a lot of the world, and I bet you can't talk about it."

"That's right. Most of the time, I can't say where I'm

going or where I've been. It's safer for everyone involved." *Especially this time.*

"I've never dated a guy in the military, but I've fantasized about it." She sighed, faking a swoon, one hand going up to land dramatically over her eyes.

Trent laughed. "It's not nearly as exciting as a romance novel, I can tell you that. In fact, it's very difficult to maintain any kind of relationship. I never know when I might be called away or how long I might be gone. Most women can't handle that in the end. They go into a relationship with all these romantic notions, but after a few months, they find themselves lonely and dissatisfied. It rarely works out."

"Is that why you're single?"

"Mostly," he admitted, glancing down. *That and the fact that I've been pining after your roommate like a loon for half my life.* If he were honest with himself, he shouldn't even be pursuing Destiny now. She'd already lost one man to the casualties of war. Expecting her to start dating another guy in the military was almost cruel.

"Destiny is strong, you know. She can handle anything." Libby's tone turned serious.

Trent didn't respond. He couldn't really know if that was true or not. He'd spent so many years ignoring her that he wasn't sure what kind of stuff she was made of anymore. All he could do was hope Libby was right, because he didn't have the strength to deny Destiny.

CHAPTER 5

Destiny was nervous. She didn't think it was warranted, but she couldn't stop shaking as she showered, dressed, and met her gaze in the bathroom mirror for a little pep talk.

"It's Trent," she told herself. "You know him better than anyone alive. Even after twelve years, he's still the same guy. There's no reason to be freaking out."

She was, though. Freaking out. After all, she had made the choice, for good or for bad, to drink too much tequila and bare her soul to her childhood friend. It hadn't entirely been an accident. The things she'd said had been on the tip of her tongue for years. She'd rehearsed what she might say to him dozens of times. All she'd needed to face him was the fortification of a few too many drinks, and *bam*.

It was surreal to think he was in her condo. Downstairs right now. Talking to her roommate. Destiny wasn't worried about what Libby would say. Trent already knew Destiny's biggest secret. If Libby inadvertently told him something, it shouldn't shock him.

Libby was a force to be reckoned with. If she was grilling Trent, fine. She could debrief Destiny later.

She took a deep breath and quickly applied minimal makeup and let her hair down from her tight bun. It fell in long thick waves down her back. The weight of her hair would quickly overcome the twists from the bun.

She had no idea where Trent intended to take her, but judging from his jeans, white button-down, and loafers, she decided to mirror him with jeans, a tight black camisole, and strappy black wedges. Something she could wear equally to a movie or a nice restaurant. She covered the camisole with a delicate, sleeveless lacy black overlay that hung down to her waist.

This was her go-to date outfit. The one that made her feel confident and sexy. She had always been slender, and no amount of eating changed that, but she did have nice boobs, and she could work it when she felt like it with a fantastic pushup bra under the tight black Lycra. The overlay just added a little mystery.

When he'd called last night, she'd originally suggested he just come to her apartment and they could order in, but he'd convinced her that there was no chance anyone they knew would see them in public in such a large city. Logically, she knew he was right. Any time he came to Dallas, they could safely go out in public. If she went to Killeen though, she hoped he would respect her desire to remain secretive.

Finally satisfied with her appearance, though still

nervous and shaking, she headed downstairs. Hopefully, she wouldn't trip and fall.

When she stepped into the living room, she found Libby sitting in the corner of the loveseat with her legs curled under her. Trent was on the sofa, leaning back and laughing at something Libby had said.

He looked like he belonged.

Not noticing Destiny's arrival, Libby continued talking. "And then there was the guy who showed up here wearing head-to-toe black leather. I kid you not. He came on his motorcycle and was carrying a spare helmet. *I* thought the guy was smokin' hot, but leather and motorcycles aren't Destiny's thing. Her eyes bugged out of her head when she saw him."

Destiny cleared her throat. *Okay, so maybe Libby could possibly share too much.* "What the heck are you telling him?" she asked, uncertain if she wanted the answer.

Trent turned toward Destiny, his eye dancing with laughter. Instantly, his face changed, growing serious. He rose slowly to his feet and wiped his hands on his thighs. "Des…" *God, the way he says my name.* It had always gotten to her, and now was no exception.

She felt self-conscious all of a sudden, not sure why he sobered so quickly. Did she have a smudge of mascara running down her face? Nope. That wasn't possible. She'd just taken a last look in the mirror moments ago. Words wouldn't come out as she held his gaze, taking in his broad shoulders and muscular thighs. The short-sleeved, white button-down made his skin look darker. The bulge of his leg muscles stretched the denim tight. He was every bit as sexy as he'd been when she first realized she had a thing for him over a decade ago. Perhaps more so.

"Yeah, that's my cue to leave." Libby jumped up from the couch and rushed past Destiny toward the stairs. "I'll just be in my room."

Trent ignored Libby as he closed the distance, coming closer and closer to Destiny as if in slow motion.

"Do I look okay for wherever we're going?" she stammered.

"Do you look okay?" He chuckled. Finally, he was in her space, one hand sliding around to her back while the other threaded into her hair at the back of her head. "You take my breath away, Des," he whispered a moment before his lips descended.

He took *her* breath away when he kissed her as if they'd done so thousands of times before but had just reunited after a long separation.

She melted into him, her hands going to his ass. Tingles rushed through her body as he slid his tongue along hers, spread his fingers over her back, and tugged her hair just enough to angle her head exactly where he wanted it.

A moan vibrated through her, and she shivered with embarrassment as she realized it came from her. She was panting when he finally broke the kiss.

He didn't pull back more than an inch, however, his intense gaze holding hers as he searched her soul. Seconds ticked by, but the silence wasn't awkward. It was perfect. As if they needed some time to remember what they meant to each other.

Destiny finally tipped her head down, unable to handle the intensity. Half of her wanted to forgo dinner and drag him up to her room to skip all the pleasantries and go right to the part where they got naked together for the first time. She wouldn't do it, but God, she wanted to.

"That was..." he murmured.

"Yeah. It was."

"We should go before I decide ordering takeout is a better plan."

"Yeah," she repeated.

His hands slid around to her waist.

When she tipped her head back to meet his gaze again, she found the same serious expression, his eyes slightly narrowed. His lips slowly turned upward. "Or we could stand here all night and stare at each other."

"That's not a bad idea, either."

He finally groaned, released her, and took a step back. After a deep breath, he turned and headed for the door. "I didn't come on a motorcycle. I hope that's okay."

She sighed. "Did Libby give you a play-by-play of *every* date I've ever been on?"

"Most of them, but then you walked in." He smiled as he opened the door. "Don't worry. It was entertaining. I like her. She's so full of personality."

"That's an understatement. Did she ask you to set her up with one of your teammates yet? She's been dying to go out with a military guy for years."

"She didn't come right out and say it, but I know the look. That starry-eyed one that tells me a woman has romanticized the life of a military girlfriend. I tried to at least give her a dose of reality, but I'm not sure she heard me. If she's serious, I know plenty of guys who would be happy to take her out." He grinned.

Destiny rolled her eyes. "If you start down that path, you'll be setting all my girlfriends up with your friends. Christa and Bex and Shayla would be jealous."

Trent laughed, his eyes crinkling. "Well, I'm sure I can come up with an unlimited supply of dates."

Destiny groaned as she followed Trent out the door. He placed his hand on her lower back as he led her to his car. When they reached the passenger side, he opened it and then leaned in to toss his duffel bag into the back seat.

Destiny took several cleansing breaths after she settled in the seat while Trent rounded the car. Of course, he had a bag with him. He was staying the weekend. They hadn't discussed anything past dinner, however, so she had no idea if he planned to sleep in her condo or even in her bed. She also wasn't sure how she felt about that.

Naturally, she wanted him in her bed. Every cell in her body wanted to find out how it felt to be naked in his arms. What kind of lover would he be? Would he be gentle and caring or rough and demanding? She couldn't imagine him being selfish, at least not with her. But one never knew.

"Relax," Trent said after he settled in the driver's seat. He reached for her hand, threaded their fingers together, and set their combined palms on his thigh. "I found a small, family-owned, out-of-the-way restaurant. No one we've ever met will see us."

She swallowed. "That's not why I'm uneasy. There's a lot of energy between us. It's powerful and it makes me nervous."

He faced her. "I know, Des, but it's always been there. The only difference is that we both know we're going to act on it. I want you to stop worrying about when. Right now, we're going to dinner. Let's take things one minute at a time. It's just a date like any other date."

She giggled indelicately. "This is not like any date I've ever been on."

He lifted their combined hands and kissed her knuckles. "Why not?" he teased, his eyes laughing again when he looked at her.

"I've never felt such an overwhelming urge to drag a man up the stairs as soon as he arrived, dinner be damned," she boldly pointed out so he would know exactly what page she was on. "However," she continued before giving him a chance to respond, "I want you to know that no matter how badly I'd love to rush things between us and skip to wild, naked sex, I won't let myself do it. I think we need to slow down, get to know each other all over again, be sure of our feelings before we make rash decisions that might make Christmases and other holidays more awkward than they've already been for the last twelve years."

He smiled at her and reached across with his free hand to stroke her face. "First of all, I'm glad you don't usually drag your dates upstairs before dinner. I'd rather not picture you with other men. And second of all, as much as I'd also love to skip to the wild, naked sex part as you call it, I agree. We should take our time."

She licked her lips. Thank God they were on the same page, even if he was just humoring her.

Trent leaned in and kissed her gently. "That being said, we only have two days together, and I have no idea when we might see each other again, so I'd really like to spend every second with you. Please tell me you'll let me sleep in your bed. I promise I won't pressure you to have sex. I just want to be with you. Or, if you're uncomfortable with me staying in your condo with your roommate there, we can get a hotel room."

She tipped her cheek into his palm. "I'd love for you to stay with me, if it doesn't bother you that I have a roommate across the hall. We have our own en suite bathrooms. It's not a problem. If we got a hotel room, well, you heard her. Libby's imagination would run rampant, and she'd make up all kinds of stories to tell our friends."

He chuckled. "We wouldn't want that. It's settled then. We're going to dinner. I'm staying in your condo. We're not having sex. Will you relax now?"

"Not a chance. I'm not sure I'll ever be able to be near you and not feel the sizzle of electricity coursing through my body right now. But, I appreciate that we settled the important stuff. At least we put our cards on the table. Now I won't spend the entire meal wondering if you're thinking about how fast you can get my clothes off after dinner."

Trent fixed her with a wicked smile. "Oh, Des, nothing is going to prevent me from thinking about peeling those fucking sexy jeans and that skin-tight, stretchy fabric off your body. I'll be wondering what's underneath the outer layers all night." He placed a hand on his heart and his expression went mock-serious. "But I'm a man of my word. I'll keep my pants on when we get back here."

She smiled and kissed his palm, uncertain if she really wanted him to be so resolved. It was the right choice, and her brain told her to tread carefully, but her heart told her to screw proprieties and let him fuck her right now into tomorrow. Because she sensed that's what would happen between them. The sexual tension was so high, it was a wonder the earth wasn't shaking.

Trent finally let her go and started his car.

She shifted her gaze to face the passenger window, needing a moment to pull herself back together. She couldn't think straight when she was looking at him.

CHAPTER 6

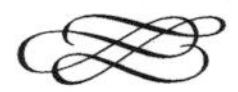

Three hours later, Trent followed Destiny back into her condo. This time, he had his duffel bag slung over his shoulder. The inside was dark, and Destiny told him Libby had mentioned going out with some of their other friends.

She turned around to walk backwards toward the stairs. "It seems absurd to pretend we're going to waste time watching TV or something. Can we just go to my room?"

"Yes." He crowded her as she reached the stairs, flattening his body against hers. He slid his hands to her waist and met her gaze. "Dinner was amazing. Best date of my life, hands down. I don't want it to end. I want you to talk to me for hours. But I'd like to do so on your bed with you in my arms. Okay?"

"Yes." That one word came out deliciously breathy. She turned around in his arms and climbed the stairs.

He kept his hands on her waist, admiring her fantastic ass as they ascended. Upstairs, he noticed there were only two doors, and Destiny opened the one on the right. "It's like two master suites," she told him.

He shut the door behind him and dropped his duffel while she made her way across the room in the near-darkness and turned on a small lamp by the bed. The dim lighting was perfect.

Trent approached, kicking off his shoes. Destiny was fidgeting, shifting her weight from side to side and rubbing her palms on her thighs. When he reached her, he grabbed her waist, lifted her off the ground, and took her with him as he fell onto his side on her bed with a huge bounce.

She giggled.

He smoothed her hair from her face as they lay side by side facing each other. *God, she's gorgeous.* "Relax. It's me. Let me hold you. Let me kiss you. I want nothing more than to listen to your voice until we can't keep our eyes open another second."

"'K." She ran her palm up his side and rested it on his hip, the feel of her fingers so very right. "I enjoy your voice, too. I missed hearing it. Sometimes, over the years, I would forget what you sounded like. I wished I had a message saved in my phone so I could hear your voice when I was particularly melancholy. Is that cheesy?"

"Not at all. I think it's nice. In fact, I'll call you tomorrow, and you can let it go to voicemail so I can leave you a message. The next time you're missing me, you'll have that."

She nodded. "I'd love that." Her voice was thick with emotion. After a few seconds, she spoke again. "You're sure this isn't weird? I mean you and me? I keep telling myself it's fine. I've wanted this for so long. But I can't help also thinking about your brother and if he's looking down on us in disappointment."

Trent closed his eyes. He hated bringing Sean into this room, but he also understood where she was coming from. "I miss him every day, Des. So much, it hurts. It never gets easier. But he would have wanted us to be happy. To move on. Even if that meant we did so together."

"You can't know that."

Oh, but I do. There was no way he was going to share Sean's letter with her just yet. He wasn't ready. Neither was she. Too much heavy emotion already filled the room. "I knew him better than anyone, and even though he was the more serious of the two of us, the introverted one who didn't say much, inside I know he loved us both."

She nodded slowly. "You're right. It's just...weird. To finally have you here, in my room, staring into my eyes. I've dreamed of a day like this for years. No matter who I dated, I couldn't fully let myself fall for him because a part of me was always yours."

He rubbed her cheek with his thumb. "I know, Des. I wish I'd seen the signs years ago. I'm sorry I wasted so many years thinking you were pushing me away because I was a reminder to you that you'd lost Sean."

"I'm a horrible person."

"You're not." He smiled at her. "You're human. We were young. When it came to you, Sean was pushy. He was also kind of desperate, I think. He asked you to marry him without thinking it through."

"Did he tell you that?" Her brows drew together.

"Not in so many words. Not out loud, but I think that's what happened."

"I'm not sure I would have been strong enough to break up with him. I might have gone through with the wedding and spent my life living with the wrong brother." She looked down.

"Des, stop beating yourself up. It's over. It's in the past. I'm here now. Plus, it's been a long time. You might not even like me anymore. You've romanticized me. I've done the same thing. We need to get to know each other again. We're adults now. A lot of life has happened since we last spoke more than a few words."

He was spouting clichés, but the intensity of feelings coursing through Trent's body brought him emotionally to his knees. This was Destiny in his arms. Right here, now. Not a figment of his imagination. She was finally his. Maybe he was crazy for thinking that, but he could sense it in his bones. He never wanted to let her go again.

And yet, he only had two nights before he had to go back to base and she had to travel all over the country for her job. He had no idea when he might see her next. He couldn't fathom what their future was going to look like. All he knew was that she was finally in his life the way he wanted, and he would not fuck this up.

Time to lighten the mood and change the subject. "What made you decide to become a flight attendant?"

She drew in a breath, visibly shaking off her

melancholy. "Honestly, I think I've been running. Running for twelve years. After Sean died, I had to get out of Killeen. I couldn't stand seeing everyone all the time. The entire town looked at me with so much sorrow. Your parents, especially your mom. God. I think her heart broke more than anyone's. Not just for the loss of her son, but she felt like she lost a daughter, too. I could see it in her eyes. I thought she was going to melt down when I told her I was moving to Dallas."

"Yeah, I agree. She was torn up. She's stronger now."

Destiny absently stroked her hand up and down his hip. "She is, but she worries about you. All the time. There's fear in her eyes whenever I see her, and I imagine that's constant. I don't blame her. I can't imagine losing a son and dealing with the fact that the other one also has a very dangerous job." Her voice dipped low as she finished, and her gaze shifted to his chest.

"You worry, too." His chest seized. This was his greatest fear. That Destiny wouldn't be able to handle another serious relationship with a man dedicated to the military.

"Yeah."

"I can't change the fact that my job is secretive and dangerous. And I won't sugarcoat it for you, either. But I will tell you that I'm good at what I do, and I never take unnecessary risks. I'll do everything in my power to ensure I always come home to you after a mission." Trent knew he was getting ahead of himself. In his mind, this relationship was lightyears ahead of real time. They were going to take the time to get reacquainted with each other, but he knew in his heart where this ended.

His chest ached as he forced himself not to think about what had happened in Kazarus. Never before had the end of a mission left lingering effects that threatened him in any way. He protected people. He rescued people. He saved lives. He usually got in, did the job, and got out. This time, things had not gone according to plan. This time, he'd come home with a weight on his shoulders. He would not let that shit touch Destiny. He couldn't. She didn't deserve the added worry. Hell, she didn't deserve him bringing this shit to her door.

A lump formed in his throat. He shouldn't even be here. He should've had the balls to put her off, knowing trouble might be lurking close to home.

When Destiny lifted her face, her eyes were watery. "Can we talk about something less maudlin?" She forced a smile.

He agreed, his thumb sliding to her bottom lip. He didn't have the strength to stay away. He needed to know if they still had the same spark they'd felt in high school. So far, the answer was a resounding *yes*. "You mean like how I'm about to kiss you senseless until you forget the stuff we can't change and focus on how damn good we are together?"

She shrugged. "It's a start," she teased.

He jerked his hand to her waist, tickled her side until she giggled and squirmed, and then he flattened her to her back, tossed a leg over both of hers, and lowered his face to take her lips.

Damn, he loved kissing her. She opened to him immediately, her tongue meeting his stroke for stroke. She tasted like a combination of the glass of white wine she'd had with dinner and the breath mint she'd picked up on the way out.

Her fingers trailed around to slide into his back pocket, and she relaxed beneath him.

Trent gripped her waist, then his hand slid up under the thin lacy thing she wore so he could palm her through the tight stretchy black camisole. He wanted more. He wanted everything. But he forced himself to stop when his thumb grazed the bottom swell of her breast.

His cock stiffened against her hip, and there was no way to hide his reaction. He wanted to inch his hand higher and cup her breast. He wanted to tug this shirt off her and yank the bra cup down so he could taste her tit. He wanted everything. But he wouldn't let himself rush this. Not tonight.

Tonight, he would focus on ensuring she knew she belonged to him in every way. Emotionally and physically. He could make her body hum without hitting any of the most sensitive parts directly. He already was. She squirmed beneath him as he pressed his thigh tighter against her and teased her breast ever so slightly with his thumb.

When she moaned, he eased his leg back, nudged hers apart, and situated his knee between her thighs. She gasped, breaking the kiss and tipping her head back until the smooth skin of her neck was exposed to his gaze. She tugged her hand out of his pocket and slid it up his torso, gripping him hard.

He pressed his thigh against her pussy, making her shudder in a way that pleased him immensely. If she responded to him like this with their clothes on, he could only imagine how she was going to light up when he got her naked and wrapped his lips around her clit.

His dick was so hard now that it pressed uncomfortably against his jeans. It was going to be disappointed tonight though. His jeans were not coming off.

"Jesus, Trent…" she breathed. She wiggled against him, lifting her hips to make better contact with his thigh.

He watched her, loving how alive she was in his arms. Her chest rose and fell. Her head was tipped back still, her eyes closed. Her mouth was open, and she breathed heavily.

When she arched her chest, he almost lost his resolve. Damn, her breasts enticed him to the point of pain. He glanced at their full swell cupped by her tight shirt. He couldn't wait to find out what her nipples looked like.

Truthfully, he was doing very little. Simply holding her, his thumb sliding back and forth beneath her breast, his thigh pressing against her heated pussy. But she squirmed as if she were close to orgasm.

He couldn't take it another second. He wouldn't take her clothes off, or his own, but God, he also wasn't about to leave her writhing like this without release. He lifted his self-imposed boob ban and slid his hand up to capture her swollen breast in his palm, molding it roughly while flicking his thumb over her nipple.

She whimpered, her hips lifting and lowering rapidly against his thigh. *She's the most gorgeous woman on earth*. Raw. Open. Sexy as hell. Even with clothes on, he was mesmerized.

He released her breast, pulled his thigh back, and dropped his hand to cup her sex.

She cried out incoherently.

He gripped her pussy through the denim, pressing his palm into her clit. Her damn jeans were wet from her arousal. The heat against his palm was enough to unman him. He rubbed her frantically, his gaze on her face as her breath hitched over and over.

The grip she had on his side would leave bruises on a normal man. He didn't have enough body fat for that, but he loved how she was so unaware of the demands she placed on him without words.

"Trent," she screamed. Her entire body went stiff a moment before she pulsed against his hand. She thrust against him and he swore he could actually feel the waves of her release even though he was probably imagining it.

It was the most amazing thing he'd ever experienced.

CHAPTER 7

Destiny couldn't breathe. It was like all the oxygen had been sucked from the room the moment Trent had cupped her breast and taken control of her body.

She was still gasping for air as she turned to putty and melted into the mattress. His hand finally slid from her sex to her waist, and his lips landed on her neck to nibble a path toward her ear. "That was the most beautiful thing I've ever witnessed, Des. Thank you."

She released an uneasy chuckle, dropping her head finally and opening her eyes to meet his gaze. "I can't believe I just did that."

"Did what?" he teased.

She swatted at his biceps as her cheeks flamed. "I'm not normally this easy."

"What do you mean? You still have your clothes on, don't you? I don't think you're easy at all." His face was filled with mirth. He wasn't displeased. That was for sure.

She groaned. "Not *that* kind of easy. I mean I don't come like that. Ever. It takes a bit of effort."

"There was effort. If I recall, I kissed you until you melted, then I tormented your breast until you squirmed, then I pressed my thigh against your pussy until you needed to grind against me to increase the pressure, and then I—"

She slapped her hand over his mouth. "I was right here, Trent. I don't need the naughty play-by-play. I get it. You made me come through my jeans. That's pretty crazy shit."

He wiggled free of her hand, kissed the corner of her mouth, and then licked the curve of her lips before drawing back. "It was fucking sexy, and I'm going to enjoy doing that to you often now that I know how easy you are," he teased.

She felt a bit embarrassed. She scrunched up her face.

He laughed. "Do you think I can do that in the car, or while we're in line to buy movie tickets, or under the table at a restaurant?"

She pressed against his shoulder. "Stop. Jeez."

He sobered, and when she met his gaze again, she swallowed back a lifetime of emotion.

"Like I said, it was beautiful, Des. Don't be embarrassed." He stroked her face, brushing back a lock of hair. "If it makes you feel any better, I promise that if I let you touch my cock right now through my jeans, I would come even faster than you just did and lose my man card."

She grinned. It was a good idea. But when she started to lower her hand, he gripped her wrist. "Not a chance, gorgeous."

"Why not? It's only fair. You made me come. Let me return the favor."

He shook his head. "Nope. Not this time."

She furrowed her brow, confused. "Trent?"

"I didn't walk into your bedroom intending to go that far. Hell, I didn't really think through the fact that we could practically have sex without removing any clothes. I should have. The sparks between us have been tingling on my skin for the past two weeks. I should've realized it would be this way. But I've already pushed you further than I should have. I said we wouldn't have sex, and then I lost my resolve and you gave me a precious gift. There is no quid pro quo though. I never want you to feel like our orgasms need to be even. They won't be. Not ever. So, don't keep a tally because I'll make you lose track of how far ahead you are so fast you won't know how many digits are between us. Got it?"

She couldn't breathe. *What on earth did he just say?*

He read the shocked, confused expression on her face. "You heard me. I will never take without giving. Never. And you can't possibly grasp how fucking hot it is to watch you come. Sure, eventually we'll have sex, and it'll be amazing, but in the end, I'll come once and spend the rest of every single time we're together making you come so many times you can't think straight."

She slowly shook her head. "That's a lot of pressure, Trent. I don't usually orgasm more than once."

He lifted both brows and slowly smiled. "Oh, baby, those days are over."

CHAPTER 8

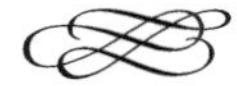

Trent had expected them to at least remove some layers of clothing before they eventually fell asleep, but that wasn't going to be possible now. The temptation would be out of control. He finally did release his grip on her to let her use the bathroom, and then he did the same. When they returned to the bed, he hauled her fully clothed body against his chest, spooning her back from behind, and kissed her neck. "Maybe tomorrow night you can change into a T-shirt or something, but not tonight."

"'K." She didn't argue. She relaxed into his embrace, her fingers dancing lightly along his forearm. "Just so you know, uh, that was… I don't come like that. I mean…"

"Des?"

"No one else has ever made me come without my help," she finally blurted out.

He flinched. "Seriously? Not even Sean?" He regretted that question the moment the words were out of his mouth. He should never bring Sean into their bed. It was crass. He didn't need—nor did he want—to know the details of her sexual relationship with his brother.

She jerked free of his grip, sat straight up, and twisted around to stare down at him.

"I'm so damn sorry. That was the stupidest thing I could have said. Please don't answer. I swear I won't mention my brother in our bed ever again." He felt like an ass. His heart was pounding so hard. He'd give anything to take back his words.

Destiny stared at him strangely though, and finally she licked her lips and took a breath. "Chill. It's okay. Let me clear the air."

He shook his head. "Nope. No air clearing necessary. Not another word."

She leaned over him, her hand landing on his arm as she met his gaze, obviously intent to say whatever was on her mind. "Trent, I never had sex with Sean. We never made it past second base. Every time we made-out, we just fumbled around. He never saw me naked. I never saw him naked."

Trent stopped breathing. He couldn't believe what she said. His brother had proposed to Destiny without sleeping with her?

"I realized much later that our awkwardness stemmed from the fact that though I loved him, he was more like a brother than a boyfriend. The physical connection wasn't there. I was too young to know that at the time. It took me several years to figure it out, and then I had a new problem."

Trent couldn't speak. All he could do was lift a brow.

"I was so enamored with another man, that I couldn't let my guard down and fully share myself with anyone."

"Another man?" he asked, his brain broken.

She smiled and poked his chest. "You, stupid."

Right. Duh. "You've had sex though, right?" he asked, his voice cracking.

"Yes. I've had sex. Just not good sex. Not sex with someone I loved. Not sex with anyone I could fully relax with. Nothing like what we just did." Her gaze was penetrating, and the weight of her words melted his heart.

She was so totally his. If it weren't absurdly too soon, he would tell her how he felt right this second. Instead, he grabbed her and pulled her close, chest to chest this time. He buried his face in her hair and inhaled her vanilla scent.

"Now that I've shared nearly every detail of my sexual experiences or lack thereof, could you please maybe not bring up the past again? Let's leave previous lovers out of our bed, yeah?"

"Absolutely." He held her tight for several more minutes and then finally loosened his grip and turned her around so that he spooned her again. He ran his hand up and down her arm, enjoying the feel of her.

He slept better than he ever had in his life.

CHAPTER 9

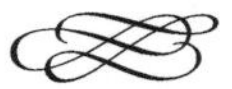

Thin rays of sunlight were filtering between the slats of blinds when Trent next opened his eyes. For a fraction of a second, he felt so peaceful. He was still holding Destiny in his arms as she softly snored. But then reality crept in when he realized what had woken him up. He squeezed his eyes closed and willed his ringing phone to be in his imagination.

It was rare for them to get called out on a mission so soon after returning, but it wasn't unheard of. He was also over two hours from base. He would have to haul ass if they needed him back.

Stifling a groan, he eased himself away from Destiny's warm body and slid off the other side of the bed. He grabbed his phone from the nightstand and then tiptoed from the room before connecting. He noted Libby's bedroom door was closed as he made his way down the stairs.

"Zip?" The voice belonged to Duff.

"Yep," he whispered, not wanting to raise his voice

until he got out of earshot. Finally, he spoke normally when he hit the ground floor and noted he was alone. "Talk to me."

"Problem."

Typical, to-the-point Gruff Duff. Trent rubbed his temples with one hand and inhaled slowly. "We always have a problem. What's new?"

"Most of our problems are on the other side of the earth. Not this time."

"Please tell me this doesn't have anything to do with blowback from Kazarus."

Duff sighed. "Sorry, man. Intel says Onur planted someone in the U.S."

"Fuck." Now he ran a hand over the top of his head. He didn't need this problem. "Do we know who?"

"Yeah. His brother, Farid Demir. He landed in New York last night. Wasn't even on a watch list. No one expected this."

Fuck. Fuck fuck fuck. "I'll be back there in two and a half hours."

"Negative. Stay there. Lie low in Dallas for the rest of the weekend. Don't change your plans. We'll get a better fix on Farid's location before you get back to base Sunday night. Deal with the threat Monday morning. Just called to give you a heads up. Stay diligent. Maybe don't go clubbing tonight." Duff chuckled, his deep burly voice ringing in Trent's ear. "Enjoy your woman. You deserve some downtime."

Trent winced. He wasn't at all positive Destiny was his woman yet. Last night, he'd fully intended to find a way to convince her.

That was before. Now, he realized he'd been selfish. There was no way he could ever be the sort of man she deserved. The sort that was available and didn't get killed.

Even though he now knew she hadn't been as head over heels in love with Sean as the world believed, she'd still grieved his loss. She'd loved him. She might not survive another loss like that.

The closer he got to her, the harder it would be on her if something happened to him. This was why he'd never gotten serious with a woman in the first place. Or maybe he was lying to himself even now. Maybe the real reason he hadn't found anyone to share his life with was that none of them were Destiny.

Nevertheless, he would not put her life in danger, and the fact that some asshole possibly had a hit out on his life was proof that he wasn't invincible either. His job was dangerous. Every Delta knew the stakes. The risks. The possibilities. What they didn't usually encounter was blowback that came home with them from a mission. That was unheard of.

And yet, it had happened. The same damn day he'd reconnected with the woman he'd been half in love with since he was a teenager.

The timing was crap.

"Zip? You there?"

"Yeah. I'll be back in a few hours."

Duff paused a second. "I get it. I do. I'd probably do the same. But you just got there with your woman."

In more ways than one. But Trent said, "This is the job, man. I knew that when I signed on." He ended the call, set his hands on the counter, and ducked his head. *Fuck.*

He wasn't about to let his shit touch Destiny. She didn't deserve it. Nor did he want her to find out about this new development. She'd worry. *Nope.* He wouldn't alarm her. Hopefully, he and his team could suppress the threat quickly and quietly without anyone on U.S. soil getting involved, especially Destiny. In the meantime, he needed to distance himself from her to keep her safe and to stay diligent.

He'd only been there one night. There was very little chance anyone had followed him. Whoever had been sent to hunt him down hadn't even landed until after Trent arrived in Dallas. He could return to Killeen without Farid Demir figuring out he had anyone special in his life. Ever.

Fuck. He slammed his palms down and cursed the universe. He'd given Destiny all sorts of shit for wanting to keep their relationship private and secretive. Yesterday, he'd wanted to climb a mountain and shout about his feelings for her to the world. Now, he needed to bow out gracefully.

He closed his eyes and gritted his teeth. At least her way would play in his favor. All he needed to do was make her think he totally agreed and use her hibernation in his favor.

This will work. It had to. And he prayed to God they'd find Farid quickly and silence him. Permanently. Of course, if Trent's Delta Team managed to take out Onur Demir's brother, that would only infuriate him more and possibly raise the stakes.

Yeah, Trent had to get back to base.

Decision made, he set about the task of making coffee. It only took him a few moments to locate the Keurig and K-cups. Luckily, Destiny didn't come downstairs while the coffee brewed. He needed a few minutes to figure out what he was going to say that wouldn't piss her off or break her heart.

Life sucked.

CHAPTER 10

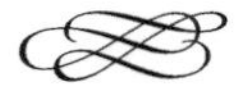

Destiny rolled onto her back and blinked up at the ceiling, her mind slowly catching up with her as she came awake. She was fully dressed in last night's clothes, but she was also overly warm from being smothered in Trent's embrace all night. Even though he wasn't in the room, she could still feel his warmth.

The smell of coffee reached her nose. She smiled. He hadn't left. He was in her condo. Making coffee. Had to be him because Libby didn't drink coffee.

Sure enough, moments later her bedroom door opened and Trent sauntered in with two mugs. He set them both down on the bedside table and then leaned over her.

"Good morning, gorgeous." He didn't quite hold her gaze.

Something was off.

"You made coffee," she murmured.

"I did. Cream and sugar. Just how you like it."

She pushed herself toward the headboard and sat

upright. He looked exactly as delicious as he had when he arrived last night. She felt gross, like she'd slept in her clothes. Which she had. And she needed a shower.

Trent apparently didn't care because he leaned forward and tucked a lock of hair behind her ear before kissing her sweetly. "I have to go," he murmured.

She sucked in a breath, meeting his gaze. There were no words. Wait, that wasn't true. There was *a* word. "Work?" She needed to make sure he wasn't sneaking out like some kind of walk of shame.

He nodded. "I'm so sorry. Something came up." He settled on the edge of the bed and reached over her thighs to rest his palm on the other side. He didn't look like a man who was running from her. *But...*

"Trent, if this was too much for you. If you're having second thoughts..."

He placed a finger on her lips. "Nope. Not even close. Best date of my life, hands down. I know this is horribly inconvenient, but it's the nature of my job. I get called on a moment's notice, and when I do, I have no choice but to drop everything and leave. Luckily, this time, I'm not scrambling around the room like a crazy man dashing for my car. They can wait for me. I said I'd be back on base in a few hours."

She swallowed back her frustration. She didn't want to come off as some kind of whiny girlfriend who couldn't handle life with a special forces operative. Yes, it was a bummer that his job could often put a damper on things, but she'd never let it show. She'd known well enough while engaged to Sean to learn to smile and keep a stiff upper lip. Dating someone in the military was hard. If she couldn't pass the early dating test, no way could she actually commit her life to him.

Besides, her job with Open Skies had similar issues when flights got canceled or delayed. She'd even used it as an excuse to break off other relationships if the guy got pissy about it.

"Will you be out of the country?" She bit her lip.

"I can't tell you that, Des."

"Yeah. I know. I shouldn't have asked. I swear I'm not going to be some clingy bitch who can't handle your job. It's just..."

He cupped her face. "I know." His voice was soft. "The timing couldn't be worse. We just got together. One date. One *amazing* date, let me add."

She set her hand on top of his. "This wasn't like some random first date. We have history. Deep feelings. We kind of rushed through the stages of dating in the first few hours. Didn't we?" Suddenly, she felt insecure.

"Yes. We totally did. It seemed like we've been together for years. I want you to know I'm on the same page, Des. No second thoughts. But I have to deal with this assignment, and I don't know how long it might take."

His expression looked too serious. His choice of words felt off.

"What are you saying? Sounds a bit like an 'it's-not-you-it's-me' speech. Why do I get the feeling you're making no commitment to contacting me for a while?"

He swallowed, his gaze lowering.

Fuck. She released his hand and jerked back as far as she could. "Trent, don't do this."

He lifted his gaze but didn't quite meet hers. "I'm not doing anything, Des. I just don't know how long I might be. Twice now I've had to leave you first thing in the morning. That's a lot of pressure on you. It's more than anyone should be expected to handle. I don't want you to put your life on hold for me. It's not fair to you."

"Fair to me?" Her voice rose. She was panicking now.

"Des…"

She shoved his arm out of the way and scrambled off the other side of the bed. After rounding it, she faced him, hands on her hips. "What the fuck, Trent?"

He reached for her waist and tugged her between his legs. "Des, don't. I didn't mean to upset you. That shit probably didn't come out quite right."

"Ya think? I'm pretty sure you just told me you might have a long assignment, and I shouldn't wait for you to come back."

"Well—"

She shook her head vehemently and grabbed his shoulders. "Did I miss something here? Did you not drive here last night, take me out to dinner, talk to me until we'd spewed out everything we'd missed in the last decade, and then give me the best orgasm of my life? Because that's what I thought was happening. I know you can't blame anything on alcohol because we both had one glass of wine. You stared into my eyes and rocked my world last night. And now you won't meet my gaze because you've got to go to work? That's bullshit, Trent."

She knew she sounded bitchy, and that pissed her off

even more. Destiny never wanted to be the kind of girlfriend who'd have a tantrum and make her man's life worse by sending him out the door for an assignment with the weight of her words on his shoulders, too. He didn't need this shit.

But what the fuck's happening here? She glanced to the side.

He slid his hands up her back and pulled her against his chest. His head tipped back. "Des, look at me."

She sighed and finally met his gaze.

"I'm not blowing you off. I just didn't want you to feel obligated to wait for me if you'd rather not. This is a harsh dose of reality. It's my life. It's not going to change. I'm in this for the long haul. It's my career. It's not fair of me to ask a woman I went on one amazing date with to put her life on hold while I fight bad guys."

She shook her head, her heart racing, a sheen of sweat breaking out on the back of her neck. "You're wrong. Don't demean what we have by pretending we're just two people who met last week and went out once. You know that's not true. If you're having second thoughts, fine. Fucking tell me. Don't put it on me. Because I'm a big girl, Trent. An adult. I can make my own fucking decisions. If the man I've lusted after for half my damn life tells me he has to go fight bad guys and do a job, I can handle that. I can wait. I waited over a decade for the first date. None of the dating I did in that time amounted to anything close to the one date I had with you last night."

Her voice cracked, and she knew she was on the edge of unwanted tears, but she had to get this out. "My feelings for you ran very deep before you arrived here. They only solidified more in the last twelve hours. I'm in this fucking thing, Trent. It's messy and inconvenient as hell, but don't—"

"Des..."

She shook her head, needing to say more. "I know I said I don't want us to tell anyone. That hasn't changed. I still don't think we should breathe a word about our relationship to anyone for a while. But that doesn't mean I don't have feelings. I'm just being cautious. If that's what's making you think I'm not interested enough to wait for you, you're wrong."

She shuddered, picturing the faces of the citizens of Killeen if they found out that 'half-black girl' who lived next to Nancy and William Dawkins had moved from one son to the other.

Nope. She wasn't ready to face anyone yet. Especially not Nancy.

"I'm in this. So, if you're not, man up and tell me. If you are, then kiss me, go do your job, and come back to me. I'm not going anywhere."

"Okay."

She heard the word but flinched anyway, her adrenaline rushing so fast she couldn't absorb his meaning.

He flattened his palms farther on her back and pulled her closer. "Okay, Des. I'm sorry. I worry. This thing between us seems too good to be true sometimes. I half-expected to arrive here last night and find that we just felt too awkward. What if we'd simply been sucked into some romanticized fantasy for twelve years?"

She rolled her eyes.

He gave her a slight shake. "The moment I stepped out of the car, I knew I wasn't making a mistake. We have something here. It's solid. I'm sorry I acted like a jackass. You're absolutely right."

"If the tables were turned and I had to go on some long-distance flight to the other side of the world and stay for two months right now, would you lose interest in me and wish you were free to date other women?"

"No. Of course not."

The tactic she'd used to shake off lesser men failed with Trent. *Thank fuck*. "Then this conversation is over. Go. Fix the world. I'll be here when you get back."

He smiled. "I don't deserve you."

"Probably not," she teased.

"I might have limited communication on this mission. Sometimes, I'm totally cut off. I don't think that will be the case. Not saying I can call every night and lull you to sleep with phone sex, but I can probably text some."

She took a deep breath, forcing a smile at his mention of phone sex. "I'll take it."

He slid his fingers up into her hair and hauled her closer until their lips met, instantly deepening the kiss so that she melted into him. He was lethal when he kissed her. She needed to remember that.

When he finally broke free, his eyes were closed, and he was panting. "I'll be back."

"I'll be here."

CHAPTER 11

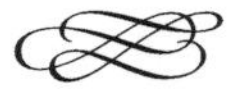

"Talk to me," Trent demanded the moment he stepped into the situation room on base. The rest of the team had already assembled, so he took the empty seat and met their gazes. Merlin and Woof were across from him. Jangles was to his left. Duff to his right.

His commanding officer, Rouvin Turano, whom they usually referred to as simply Roe, stood at the head of the table. He wiped his forehead with two fingers and met Trent's gaze. "Sorry to cut your weekend short."

Trent nodded, not wanting to think about what he'd walked away from to deal with this shit. He needed to learn to compartmentalize if he was going to enter into a serious relationship. Thoughts of Destiny would not be permitted while he was working. He had no idea how other Deltas did it, but somehow they managed. Hell, he knew for a fact both Lefty and Trigger juggled their jobs and their women. Woof was in a relationship now, too. He should talk to Woof. Get his advice. Pick his brain. *Later.*

The truth was, Trent had never imagined himself in this position. He'd never expected to enter into a serious relationship with a woman. Admittedly, now that he'd hashed things out with Destiny, he realized the reason he'd never considered marriage or even a serious long-term connection was because he'd been permanently hung up on her. And, as far as he'd been concerned right up until a few weeks ago, she'd clearly not been interested, steering clear of him for a dozen years, rarely making eye contact when they did run into each other. This twist still had him reeling.

Woof turned toward Trent. "Things escalated."

"Apparently, or you wouldn't all be sitting here. Not sure why you thought I should continue to relax in Dallas while you all met to deal with this threat to my life." He was pissed, but on the other hand, he knew they'd been trying to give him a break.

Turano cleared his throat. "It was my command that you be given leave. Don't blame your team. I didn't see things escalating so quickly. Situation changed. I called everyone in. You're here now. Can we fucking move on?" He lifted a brow.

"Yes, sir." Trent needed to lose the attitude and listen to the briefing.

"Good." Roe continued. "Intelligence sources discovered something none of you are gonna like. It's important to remember that the mission was successful. None of you have any reason to doubt your actions. You rescued all the doctors and nurses from Onur Demir's compound with few casualties. However, as you all know, one of the shots fired hit the machine that was keeping Onur's son alive and the kid died. New video evidence proves that shot came from Zip's gun."

"Fuck." Trent groaned. It hadn't been intentional. The boy had simply gotten caught in the crossfire. Trent would never intentionally harm a child. Hell, he'd never even *unintentionally* involved a child, either.

Across from Trent, Merlin narrowed his blue eyes. "Don't even go there, Zip. We all know that kid was dying anyway. He was living on borrowed time."

Next to Merlin, Woof set his elbows on the table. "He's right, Zip. It didn't matter that Demir's army kidnapped those doctors in an effort to save his kid's life. None of them had been able to accomplish anything. The kid was too sick, the leukemia too far gone. He was basically already dead. He wasn't even conscious. He never even knew he'd stopped breathing."

Trent knew they were all trying to take away the sting from his mistake, but he still felt the weight of the responsibility. Maybe the kid would have died sooner or later, but he didn't like being the one who delivered the final blow. "Fuck."

"Shake it off," Roe demanded. "Our concern now is that Demir recorded everything in that room. All he had to do was slow down the video and he knew exactly who fired the shot that hit the machinery."

"Are we certain it's his own brother, Farid, he sent to do his dirty work?" Jangles asked as he ran a hand over his blond hair.

Roe nodded. "Either that or someone posing as Farid. The description is in line with what we know." Roe set his hands on the table and leaned forward.

"Until we know more, there is nothing we can do. Stay alert. Watch your backs. You know the drill. Business as usual."

Trent fought the urge to roll his eyes. He was never disrespectful to his commanding officer, but he knew as well as everyone in the room that it was his ass on the line here. Not theirs.

Roe continued. "Zip, you live in the same apartment building as Woof. You don't leave the apartment without having him at your six."

"Got it." He hated it, but he got it.

"I suspect Farid Demir will take his time. Watch you like a hawk when he finds you. Wait to make his move. His goal has to be to take you out."

Trent hated the matter-of-fact way Roe so flippantly referred to his life, but it was to be expected.

Roe shoved away from the table and headed for the door. He turned back to face the room. "Your team won't be assigned to another mission until this situation is resolved. Until then, *this* is your mission."

"Yes, sir," they all responded in unison.

CHAPTER 12

One week later…

Trent was climbing out of his skin. He'd never spent so much time inside his apartment in his life. Not this one or any other. He was the kind of guy who would go to the store just to pick up three things as an excuse to be moving and doing something. He didn't appreciate living in his new Fortress of Solitude.

The rest of his team seemed to have put together a schedule to keep him occupied. They stopped by at regular intervals. Woof or Jangles often in the mornings. Merlin or Duff in the afternoons.

Trent was known among the group for his outgoing positive personality. He was usually the first to crack a joke or lighten the mood. After seven days of being sequestered for long hours in his apartment, he was losing his patience. Worse, he knew they could all sense it. His attitude shift had made them all regard him with concern.

Hell, he'd even come to realize one of the reasons he was probably as easygoing as he'd been labeled was the result of years of faking like his life was rosy and perfect without a woman in it. Specifically one woman. He'd never admitted that consciously, even to himself, but there was some merit to the acknowledgment.

Now, he was actively lying to Destiny every day. He couldn't bring himself to tell her he was in Killeen instead of the Middle East or California or some other distant location. He didn't want to tell her he was in danger and worry her, and he knew if she found out he was nearby, she'd want to see him. On the flipside, he selfishly feared if she knew about the threat, she wouldn't want to have anything to do with him.

He couldn't blame her. It was one thing to know your man traveled to far-off locations for covert missions. It was another thing altogether for those missions to endanger everyone he knew right at home. In fact, the only time he'd seen his parents had been on base yesterday. They'd met him there because he didn't want to endanger them at their own house or let Destiny's grandmother see him and tell her.

Dammit. He wasn't sure how long he could carry on this ruse, lying to Destiny. He had no choice because he wouldn't risk her life, but part of him also feared she would run and never look back if she knew about this.

He wanted to see her. This damn confinement was wearing on his nerves. Every day he worried she would discover his lie and tell him to go to hell, but she would at least be safe. More than anything, he didn't want to involve her in this fucking blowback. She was innocent in his stupid mistake. Putting her life in danger was not fucking going to happen.

He'd worked out all morning lifting weights in his spare bedroom before picking up his phone to read the latest text from her. He'd gotten it yesterday, but wouldn't permit himself to respond until today. He needed her to think he was too busy or too far away.

Hey. Thinking about you. I'm in Seattle today. I'll be back in Dallas tomorrow afternoon. I have three days off. Wish you were able to spend them with me. Stay safe.

He groaned. He could hear her voice every time she texted. Frustration mounted daily. It was time to respond.

Des, got your message. That sucks. Wish I were available. I don't know how long this mission is going to take. It's dragging out. I hope your trip was smooth. I'll update you with more when I know more.

He hit send, set the phone on the coffee table, and dropped his head back, hating this situation with a passion.

A knock on the door made him take a cleansing breath and rise. He looked through the peephole to see Woof standing in the hallway. Not surprising. It was apparently his day. Trent unlocked and opened the door, and then he turned and walked toward the kitchen. “I don’t need a babysitter, you know. You guys can stop with the hovering. I’m a grown-ass man.”

“Yeah, well, we know you’re not the kind of guy who likes to be cooped up,” Woof responded as he shut the door and turned the lock.

Trent didn’t respond. He grabbed a glass, filled it with tap water, and took a long drink. Leaning his ass against the counter, he met Woof’s gaze. “Any new information?” It was a longshot. Someone would have called Trent before anyone else if there was something to say.

“No. Nothing new since intel determined the man who landed in the U.S. a week ago was for certain Onur’s brother, Farid. Surveillance videos confirmed. Same height and build. Dark hair. Dark eyes. He has a scar on his left cheek. He arrived in the U.S. alone. Didn’t even bother to use a fake passport. But you know all of this.”

Trent nodded.

Woof dropped down on one of the armchairs in Trent’s living room, his gaze shifting to the coffee table. “You have an incoming text lighting up.”

Trent shoved off the counter and padded that way. Even though the texts he exchanged with Destiny were innocuous, he still hated sharing them. These intermittent texts were all he had with her right now. He grabbed the phone and read her latest response. She would be back in Dallas today, starting her three-day break.

Trent, I'm on my way to Killeen to spend a few days with Grandma. If you happen to get back in town, you know where to find me.

She added a smiley face emoji.

Trent blew out a breath. *Great.* If she found out he was in Killeen, she would dump his ass without asking questions.

"Everything okay?" Woof asked.

"No. Everything is not fucking okay. I had one brief date with the woman I've wanted for half my life, and now I'm fucking lying to her about my location to keep her safe. She's gonna lose her shit if she finds out I'm in town. In addition, she's on her way here to visit her grandmother, which makes me fucking nervous. I can't know for sure if Farid knows I have anyone important in my life or not, but I'd rather he didn't."

Woof nodded. "I hear ya. I'd be freaking out too if I were in your shoes. No way in hell would I expose Nori to something like this. I don't think I woulda kept it from her, though. I'm not sure you should have lied to Destiny. Why not just come clean?"

Trent sighed. "Honestly, I had hoped we could find this fucker quickly and put an end to this threat. She could've gone her entire life without knowing someone had a hit on me. We've barely reached the stage in our relationship where we've expressed any feelings at all. I really didn't want our first conversation about my job to be that someone wanted me dead and was probably lurking around in town."

"Zip, man, if she's as into you as I suspect, she won't freak easily."

"That's also possible, and I'm not sure which is worse—her deciding she can't take the heat of my job or her not taking the threat seriously enough and getting herself killed in the crossfire. Either way, I would prefer she not worry needlessly about something I can't control. The entire thing infuriates me and makes me think I should never have gone out with her in the first place. I have myself half-convinced the right thing to do would be to cut her loose so she can find someone normal and have a stress-free civilian life."

Woof shook his head, but his lips were turned up slightly at the corners. "If only the heart were strong enough to pull it off. Trust me, Trent, I've been there. I'm *still* there. Nori is the one halfway around the globe. I worry about her constantly. Her job is almost as dangerous as mine, sometimes more so, but I wouldn't give her up for the world. No matter what happens to either of us, I'd rather have spent every possible hour together between assignments than never see her again. Cutting her off has never been an option for me. I laid all my cards on the table and let her know how I felt. The rest is essentially up to her. But, Zip. If you don't give Destiny choices, she can't make the most informed one."

"I get it."

"So, let's find this motherfucker and take him out. Then you can clear the air, and I can get back to my previously scheduled life."

Trent smiled. "I like this plan."

CHAPTER 13

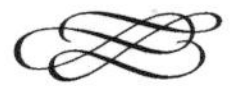

"You going to tell me what's bothering you, Des, or do I have to start guessing?"

Destiny chuckled and then wiped her lips with her napkin. She was sitting across from her grandmother at her small kitchen table. Leave it to Stella Fisher to sense something was off.

"Is it that obvious?"

"Yes." Stella picked up her cup of tea and took a sip. "You've been moping around since you got here last night. You're starting to worry me."

"Maybe I'm just having a bad week." Destiny knew her grandmother wouldn't buy that. The woman had raised her from the age of five. It had always been just the two of them. They could both read the other's moods well.

"You haven't moped like this since Sean died. I worried about you incessantly for a few years back then, but once you got more established in Dallas and developed closer friendships, you seemed to return to your old self. The woman sitting across from me right now is not happy. Is it your job? Or did you break up with a new boyfriend?" Stella prodded.

Destiny swallowed her next bite of sandwich and took a deep breath. She'd never kept things from her grandmother, except when it came to her feelings about the Dawkins brothers. She regretted thinking she needed to keep Trent from her now. She realized it wasn't necessary to leave Stella in the dark. The older woman would never breathe a word of Destiny's private life to a single soul in Killeen if Destiny asked her not to. And that included Trent's parents next door.

"Funny you should mention Sean."

Stella lifted a brow and set her elbows on the table. Sometimes it was hard for Destiny to remember her grandma was almost seventy years old. She had the wrinkles and the age marks, but other than that the woman could still run circles around most people. She had the physique of a thirty-year-old, walked two miles a day, ate healthy, and kept busy even in retirement. She didn't say a word, either. She was waiting for Destiny to continue.

"I ran into Trent a few weeks ago."

"Yeah? How is he? You never mention him anymore."

"He's good. He's..." She wasn't sure what she wanted to say or how to say it. Suddenly, she was overwhelmed with emotion. The last few weeks had been challenging. The sum total of her interactions with Trent included her spilling her heart in a drunken stupor, him confessing he also had feelings for her, and one amazing date that ended with her sleeping better than she had in years wrapped in his arms. Her daydreams about him that included fucking hot sex followed by the two of them riding off into the sunset were beyond absurd. She'd blown their relationship out of proportion. There simply wasn't anything substantial enough to it for her to get so far ahead of herself.

"Des? Hon? You okay?"

Destiny sucked back a breath, but the dam finally broke, and tears fell down her cheeks right before she gave an audible sob.

"Honey..." Stella reached across the table and grabbed both of Destiny's hands, squeezing them. "What is it? Talk to me."

"It's silly really," Destiny murmured. "I'm being ridiculous."

"I'm sure you're not. You're a bright woman with a fantastic head on her shoulders. If something's bothering you, I'm certain it's warranted. What happened with Trent?"

Destiny met her grandmother's gaze and decided to lay it all out on the table. "I think I'm in love with him. I always have been."

Stella slowly smiled. "Honey, I know that."

Destiny flinched. "What?"

Stella shrugged. "You always did have eyes for Trent. Even when you were five. He was the first one of them to catch your attention, probably because he was more outgoing and louder. He teased you mercilessly when you were kids, and you ate it up. Frankly, I was surprised when you started dating Sean, but I didn't want to get in your business."

Destiny was speechless. Shocked. She should have realized her grandma would pick up on the cues. Why hadn't anyone else? Especially Nancy, Sean and Trent's mother.

"I assume you two finally admitted you had feelings for each other?"

Destiny nodded, pulling her hands back so she could wipe her eyes with her napkin. "I kinda spilled my guts and forced a confrontation," she admitted, leaving out the part where she was drunk.

"Good for you. And what did he say?"

"He agreed, shockingly."

Stella smiled broader. "Not surprised. So, why are you so sad exactly?"

Destiny couldn't help but shake her head and chuckle. "I should have come to you years ago."

Stella lifted one shoulder. "I don't know. I'm not sure I could have been helpful. You two had to figure out your feelings on your own in your own time."

"But you suspected Trent also liked me?"

"Of course. He followed you around like a puppy for years, his gaze always on you in a crowded room. And then when you started dating Sean, he grew withdrawn and quiet. Not like himself at all. It was obvious to me, but I can understand why no one else noticed. After all, you three were inseparable. And Nancy…"

"Yeah. Nancy." Destiny smiled as she dabbed at another tear.

"Her heart is made of gold. She loves you to pieces. All she could see was that you were going to marry one of her sons. She thought of you as her own daughter for most of your life. I'm sure she was elated and didn't see what was happening right under her nose."

Stella's astuteness stunned Destiny. She had underestimated the woman.

"So, what's the problem, Des?"

Destiny's shoulders fell. "It's such a messy situation. Trent and I haven't had a chance to really get to know each other yet. My feelings are a jumbled mess of hope and happiness and nerves. I told him I didn't want anyone in town to find out about us until we were far more certain and solid."

Stella frowned. "Why would you do that?"

"I just think it's easier. People around here think I'm some sort of sad widow even though Sean and I were never even married. I'm afraid they'll gasp and gossip if they find out I'm dating his brother. It was hard enough for the town to accept that the poor little half-black girl with the dark kinky curls whose mother abandoned her was dating one of their own white boys. Lord knows what they'll say if I switch brothers."

"Destiny Fisher. Since when do you care what people think? I raised you to feel loved even without your mother or father in your life. To hold your head high. Own your heritage. Show the town you were just as good as any of them."

Destiny grinned. "You did. And I love you more than you'll ever know. I was the luckiest little girl in the world. I owe you my life. When Mom disappeared, you could have let me go into the system, but you didn't. You put your own life on hold to raise yet another child. You didn't have to do that, and I love you for it."

Stella's eyes widened. "Des, don't talk like that. You're the best thing that ever happened to me after your mother. I still miss her every day. She was such a happy, sweet child before she ran off right after high school. I hate that I'll never know what happened to her. I don't even know if she's alive or dead. I'll probably die without finding out. But then you came to me. You were like a blessing. A second chance. My own flesh and blood. And I wouldn't trade that for the world. You're the light of my life."

Destiny started crying again. "Thank you," she murmured. She tried to swallow back her emotion and continue. "It's more complicated than that—my relationship with Trent, that is. I'm worried about what his parents will think. How they might react."

"That's lunacy, Des. They love you. Nancy will be over the moon."

"And you may be right, but I really don't want to rock that boat unnecessarily. Why tell her anything and find out she either can't understand or she understands so well that she chooses a wedding venue prematurely?"

Stella's shoulders shook as she chuckled. "You're right about that last part."

Destiny smiled through her stupid tears. "I just want to take things slow and be sure before we make some sort of announcement. We haven't had a chance to get to know each other yet. If for some reason one of us just isn't feeling it, we don't need to have caused a disturbance."

Stella sighed. "I understand. I don't think it's necessary, and I don't like it, but I hear your concerns."

She leaned forward again. "Now, explain to me why you're sitting in my kitchen entertaining an old woman on your three days off instead of shacking up with the man you're pursuing?"

Destiny lost it to a fit of giggles. "*Grandma*. Shacking up?"

"Well, isn't that what you young people call it?"

She rolled her eyes. "That's so crude. But the reason I haven't seen him is because he's on an assignment. He's been gone a week."

Stella frowned. "What do you mean?" She shook her head. "He's not gone. He's here in Killeen. I just spoke to Nancy yesterday evening while I was watering my flowers. She said she and William had been over to the base earlier having lunch with him."

Destiny's heart stopped. She couldn't move a muscle. Not even to blink. *No way. It's not possible*. "Are you sure?" she whispered. "Maybe you misunderstood."

"Nope. I heard her fine. She told me he's working on some sort of secret mission right here in town. It's all very hush-hush. That's why Nancy went to Fort Hood to see him. He's too busy to come by the house."

Destiny swallowed, her mouth suddenly too dry. Trent was here in Killeen? She pulled her phone from her pocket and scrolled back to read through all of his texts. There were only about six since she'd seen him last weekend. He seemed to make a point of texting her once a day. Every communication was brief and unemotional. He'd said nothing personal, but she'd tried to convince herself that maybe he wasn't the sort to share his feelings in a text. She had taken his lead and kept her own texts short and sweet, not wanting to push him. It was too soon to make assumptions.

She read every text again. He'd never once said he was out of town. But in her last text, she'd told him she would be in Killeen. Since then, nothing.

Destiny shoved back from the table and paced the small kitchen.

"Hon, I'm sure he's working."

"Yeah." *He's also ghosting me. Dammit. Why would he do this?* Why string her along if he didn't really want to see her again? Had she pushed him last Saturday? She'd thought he was trying to back out when he told her he had to leave, but then he'd seemed so sincere when he insisted it had nothing to do with her.

But this made no sense. She couldn't think of a single reason why he would need to make her believe he was off fighting some unknown enemy when he was right here in town. Did he have no balls? *Fuck.*

As if on cue, her phone pinged on the kitchen table and she stomped over to pick it up.

Did you make it to Killeen okay? How is your grandmother?

Shit. Dammit. Fuck.

There weren't enough swear words in the English language for how pissed she was right now.

Destiny spun around and rushed from the room. She had to grasp the doorframe of her childhood bedroom to stop her momentum as she entered. She grabbed the first pair of shoes she could find and put them on. White Keds.

Not caring that her hair was in a messy ponytail today and that she had on very little makeup, a plain white T-shirt, and jeans, she grabbed her purse and keys and rushed back out to the main room.

Stella was standing in the living room, wringing her hands together. "Hon, do you think this is the best idea? He must have a reason why he hasn't told you where he is."

"I'm sure he does, and I want to hear it. In person. Now. Today."

"Okay, but be careful. You're angry. I don't want you to drive carelessly."

Destiny paused and gave her grandmother a quick hug. "I'll be fine. I promise." *Can't say the same for Trent. But I'll be perfectly peachy.*

CHAPTER 14

Trent was just dropping the empty container from his TV dinner in the trash when a knock sounded at his door. He glanced at his watch. It was two in the afternoon. He rolled his eyes as he padded toward the door, wondering why his team members were off-schedule. After all, Jangles had been there that morning, and he wasn't expecting Merlin for another few hours.

He looked through the peephole as usual and then gasped. *Shit.*

Destiny stood right outside his door. Her hands were on her hips and she was glaring at him as if she knew he would look before opening the door.

His heart pounded as he yanked the door open. "Des…" He glanced both ways down the hallway and then stepped back and ushered her inside with a hand motion.

Destiny entered his apartment, stomped right past him, dropped her purse on his coffee table, and spun around. "Surprise."

He shut the door, praying no one had seen her arrive.

"Des..." He had no idea what to say. She was clearly pissed and rightfully so. He felt like the biggest fuck alive, hating the way she was glaring at him.

She set her hands on her hips again. "Did you think I could come to town, stay with my grandmother for the weekend—the grandmother who lives next door to your parents—and not accidentally find out you were also in Killeen?"

He rubbed his hands on his jeans, trying to come up with an explanation. He should've known his mom couldn't keep from telling Stella he was in town, even after swearing her to secrecy. *Dammit. What a fucking mess.*

"Des, I'm not hiding from you. I'm working."

She rolled her eyes dramatically and groaned. "That is the lamest thing I've ever heard." She glanced around his living room and kitchen. "Working on what? Looks to me like you're having a lovely Saturday afternoon hanging out waiting for some game to come on TV. You're in jeans and a T-shirt. You don't even have shoes on. You led me to believe you were in Afghanistan or Alaska or something."

He inched closer, hating his life right about now. He'd hurt her. Badly. Possibly irreparably. Because the reality was he still couldn't tell her a thing about his current situation. *And,* to make matters worse, he needed to get rid of her before she became a target for some revenge-seeking member of the Demir family.

"I never said I was out of town," he murmured, foolishly trying to defend himself.

"Oh *please*. Give me a break. How stupid do you think I am? Why in the hell didn't you just tell me to my face last week that you weren't feeling it and you didn't want to see me again? What a coward."

He took another step closer. He was so fucked right now, but there was no way in hell he was going to allow her to believe he wasn't into her. It was so far from the truth. He'd done nothing but think about her for a week all cooped up in this damn apartment while sending her short cryptic texts that kept her at arm's length and obviously left her feeling empty and confused.

Meanwhile, they'd made very little progress locating Farid Demir. The fucker was in the wind. He'd rented a car in his real name, and that's about all anyone knew. Trent was no closer to finishing this mission than he had been a week ago. Things were worse because by now there was every possibility Farid had driven to Texas and was even right this moment staked out somewhere waiting for Trent to walk outside so he could put a bullet in Trent's head.

Destiny held out a hand. "Don't. Stay where you are. I don't need you to coddle me. I'm a grown woman. Big enough to handle this rejection. I'll leave and you won't have to hear from me again. Hell, we managed to avoid each other for twelve years without much trouble. We can just go back to doing that again. This is exactly why I didn't want to tell anyone about us. I didn't want to give anyone in town reason to gossip unnecessarily, nor hurt your mother and give her false hope. See? Don't you feel relieved we don't have to explain our breakup since we never told anyone we were dating in the first place?"

Yeah, he felt like cow shit.

She gave a sharp laugh that sent a chill down his spine. Her hands went out to her sides. "What the fuck am I even talking about? We were never dating at all. We went on one date. *One.* Whatever is happening right now can't really be considered breaking up after such a brief encounter. I'm a damn fool."

He opened his mouth, but she cut him off with another hand in the air, palm out in front of him. "Please, don't say some stupid shit that will just make you look like a bigger asshole than you already are. But let me give you some advice—the next time you go out with a woman and realize you don't want to see her again, just fucking tell her to her face. We aren't weak, you know. We're stronger than you give us credit for. We'd much rather be told straight up that you're just not that into us than be ghosted and dragged along on some sort of ride because you feel guilty, or because you're too much of a coward to look us in the eye."

After that rushed speech, Destiny grabbed her purse and headed toward the door.

Trent finally had a fire under him. He moved past her, flattened himself to the door, and stopped her. "Are you done?"

She glared at him. "Trent, this is over. Let me go."

"Des, this is so far from over, you have no idea." He kept speaking, not giving her a chance to continue.

"How about you let me respond? You at least owe me that much." He lifted a brow.

She sighed, looking bored, one hip cocked out to the side in defiance.

"I know you're pissed, and you have every right to be. I can't fault you for your assumptions because everything you've presumed makes perfect sense with what information you have. But I need you to understand something. Contrary to appearances, I *am* working. My case is local, and it's serious. I knew I would be busy around the clock while I handled this matter, so I didn't bother telling you where I would be."

She glanced around. "Trent, you don't even have a fucking computer open."

He closed his eyes and blew out a breath. She was right, and he was still lying to her. The truth was, he'd done very little besides lie low in hiding. He had spent hours online working every angle he could to ascertain where Farid Demir was. He was losing his mind and going stir-crazy. If his commander would let him, he'd rather just walk right out in broad daylight and ferret the asshole out directly.

But that would put the general public at risk, so it wasn't an option. Roe would never agree to that. He wanted Delta Force to hunt Demir down and take him out directly. Sneak up on him. So far, none of Trent's team had a single lead to follow.

"Des, I'm begging you to trust me." He met and held her gaze as his heart pounded. "Please. I can't tell you a single detail about what I'm working on. That's the nature of my job. What I can tell you is that I hate the timing. I hate that our first date got interrupted and cut short because of this case. I hate that I didn't get to spend the entire weekend with you."

Her shoulders dropped enough that he thought he was getting in there.

He softened his voice. "That was the single best night of my life, Des. Would I bother to say that if it weren't true?"

She pursed her lips, not willing to admit defeat yet.

He couldn't blame her. He had a lot of apologizing to do. "I haven't slept well since I got back here. I know we really only had fifteen hours together, but I thought we skipped through about half of the dating steps and entered into a pretty solid relationship in that time. I know I did."

She licked her lips.

"Des, you mean the world to me. You have for half my life. Nothing has changed. I'm still yours. But I belong to the Army first. I made an oath to put my country first, and that means any relationships I have, including with my own parents, sometimes have to take a back burner. It's a lot to ask of another human being, and half the reason I never dated anyone seriously was because I'm fully aware of that."

She swallowed, her body relaxing further.

"If I could ignore my feelings for you, I would. If I were a stronger man, I'd let you believe everything you surmised and walk away from me. Your life would be much less complicated and stressful without me in it." He reached out a hand, praying she would take it.

She met him halfway, touching the tips of his fingers.

He lurched forward, grabbed her palm, and tugged her against him so that her body fell into his.

She gasped as their torsos lined up.

He flattened one hand on her lower back and slid the other up into her loose ponytail. "Des, if you want an easy life without complications and a man who comes home every night at six o'clock, you need to walk out this door and never look back."

"Trent…"

"If you're willing to give up a lot of nights and weekends in a relationship with a man who can't tell you when he'll be working, how long, or where, then stay and jump on this moving train because I don't have the strength to let you walk away from me a second time. I already let you go once. I won't do it again."

She didn't say anything, but a tear slid down her face.

Trent wiped it away with his thumb. "I'm a smart guy. I know I should tell you that I've decided this isn't going to work out. I should tell you I'm not into you. Not feeling it. I should stand here and convince you I don't want to go out with you again. But I won't because I want this chance with you more than anything in the world." *Enough that I'm selfishly putting your life at risk.*

She smoothed her hands up his chest and wrapped them around the back of his neck. "I'm sorry. I jumped to conclusions."

"Don't be. I knew this might happen. I just didn't know how to manage it."

"I don't quite understand why you couldn't tell me where you were. You could have said you had a local job and wouldn't be available."

He shook his head. "I couldn't tell you that any more than I could have told you I was in the Middle East, Des. I don't have that authority. Everything I do is classified."

"Are you going to get in trouble or something because I found you?" She gave him a slight teasing grin. She also gave him the perfect opening. *This could work.*

"Not if no one finds out you were here." Granted, he was exaggerating. None of his team nor his commander would reprimand him for Destiny's appearance. It wasn't her fault. She was totally innocent. But now that she was in his apartment, he needed to be careful. He didn't want her to become a target for Farid.

She could stay until the early hours of the morning and then sneak out. He could use her unwillingness to go public with their clandestine affair to his advantage and keep her safe without mentioning a word of his current situation.

It was true that he couldn't discuss the mission, but more than that, he simply didn't want her to know how much danger he was in—that she was in, by default.

She sighed and flattened her cheek against his chest. "I overreacted."

"No. You didn't. You reacted exactly how anyone would."

"I'm not some whiney girlfriend who can't handle your job," she told his chest before lifting her face again.

"I guess evidence would suggest the contrary, but I'm not."

He smiled and tugged her ponytail. "I know you're not. You've had a lot thrown at you in a short time. I'm not going to sugarcoat things. Maintaining a relationship with me won't be roses and chocolates, but the last few weeks have been unusually unfair to you."

"I'm done being a bitch."

"You're not a bitch. But you have to trust me, Des. I know that's asking a lot after one date, but there's no other options. You have to trust that when I look you in the eye and tell you I'm committed to meandering down this path with you, it's because I truly want to. I'm not hanging on to you because I'm too cowardly to break things off. Not gonna lie, I did consider putting an end to this last weekend when I got called away, but not because I didn't want to see you again. I just hate what kind of life you're stepping into. It's not fair to you."

"I'm taking this step with my eyes wide open, Trent."

"If I don't call or I'm cryptic, know it's for a good reason."

"'K. Do you want me to leave?"

He shook his head. He definitely didn't want her to leave. What he wanted was to spend the evening with her. Now that she was here, she might as well stay. It would be safer if she left at an odd hour.

"No. I want you to stay. You can sneak out late tonight or early tomorrow morning and no one will be the wiser," he teased halfheartedly.

She smiled broader. "I'd like that."

A knock sounded at the door, and Trent snapped his

fingers. "Shit. That'll be Merlin. I was supposed to meet with him this afternoon."

Her face fell. "I can go." She reached for the door.

Trent grabbed her arm. "Not a chance." He looked through the peephole and then opened the door.

Merlin's brows went up as he glanced from Trent to Destiny.

"Destiny, this is Merlin. Merlin, Destiny."

Merlin wiped his hand on his thigh and then reached out and shook Destiny's. "Guess you don't need me this afternoon." He smirked.

"Nope." Trent knew Merlin would understand.

Merlin backed up and waved. "I'll call you tomorrow."

"Thanks, man. Appreciate it."

"You sure this is okay?" Destiny asked as Trent shut the door. "I didn't mean to interrupt if you have something you need to do."

Trent shook his head. "Positive. I'll make you dinner. We can talk. Call it date number two."

"You cook?" Her smile lit up even further.

"Of course. I'm a bachelor. I've been living on my own since I got out of high school. There's no way I could stay in good physical shape if I ate fast food every day."

She leaned back and glanced down at his chest. "Good point. And you are for sure in the best physical shape of anyone I've ever met." She smoothed her hands down his pecs and explored a bit.

God, he loved her touch. Loved the way she looked at him. Loved the feel of her hands roaming over his body. His cock jumped to attention. Now was a good time to put some space between them so he didn't end up dragging her to his bedroom.

He needed to continue to be a gentleman tonight. It wasn't fair to take their relationship further under the circumstances. She didn't have all the information.

He grabbed his phone off the counter and sent a quick text to Merlin. Trent obviously didn't need babysitting right now, but he did need someone from the team to watch his apartment when Destiny left and follow her back to her grandmother's to ensure she was safe without her finding out he was being hunted. Woof was under orders to watch Trent, or he would have texted him.

Fuck, this is a mess. He prayed they caught Farid soon. He also prayed doing so would send a message to Onur that no hitman was going to be able to reach Trent.

CHAPTER 15

Destiny hoisted herself up on Trent's counter, crossed her legs under her, and accepted the glass of white wine he handed her. "You seriously just want me to sit here and watch you cook? I could help, you know."

He grinned at her in that silly evil way that made her insides melt a little. "I know you could, but I want to do this."

"Hmm. Is this some secret thing you do to lure all the women into going out with you again? You show them your very best qualities so that they will remember those when you disappear from town for weeks at a time?" She watched as he pulled out a wok and then set a pan on another burner. He was certainly comfortable in the kitchen, and she realized there were a lot of things she didn't know about him since she hadn't given him five seconds of her time in a decade.

He smirked. "Des, if I wanted to show you my best qualities to ensure you wouldn't forget me when I'm out of town, we wouldn't have started in my kitchen."

She shivered, her lady parts jumping to attention. "Living room? You're good with an Xbox?" she joked.

He put water in the pan and turned on the burner without a word, and then he sauntered toward her, his lips turned up just slightly, his eyes hooded, his gaze boring into her.

She didn't breathe while he moved, and she didn't want to blink, either. And then he was in her space. He set his hands on her thighs and stroked upward. He leaned in slowly until his lips met hers. When he angled his head to deepen the kiss, he slid his hands up her waist and didn't hesitate a single second before he cupped her breasts and molded his palms to them.

She nearly dropped her wine glass.

The kiss was over all too quickly, and then he was backing up, leaving her bereft of his touch. She set the glass on the counter at her side with shaky hands. Suddenly, his expression changed as if a light bulb went off. He snapped his fingers, just remembering something. "Oh, that's right. I already demonstrated that side of me. You shouldn't need a reminder. It was only a week ago." He wiggled his brows as he turned toward the counter next to the stove and grabbed an onion.

Destiny's pulse had picked up considerably. *Screw dinner*. She wanted some more of that. "I'm not sure I remember every detail. Maybe you could show me again."

He glanced at her, a shit-eating grin on his face. "Oh, I will. But not on our second date. You deserve better."

She took a deep breath and picked the wine glass

back up. She needed a good long drink. She did not need a second date that ended without sex. She also didn't want him to think she was forward, so she would keep her mouth shut for now and let him set the pace.

For the next half hour, she mostly watched him work, mesmerized by how comfortable he was in the kitchen. He never looked at a recipe, and he had the chicken stir fry ready at the same time as the rice. She was impressed.

"Did you text your grandmother?" he asked as she slid off the counter to join him at the table.

"Yes. While you were texting your teammate."

"Good." He held out a chair for her. "I don't want her to worry."

"I'm sure she's pleased with herself since I left there furious while she tried to convince me you surely had a good reason for being in town and not telling me."

"She's a wise woman." Trent ladled too much food on her plate and then sat in front of his own. "Tell me about your parents." He took a bite and then lifted his gaze. "I mean, I know your mom took off when she was eighteen and never came back. I remember my mother explaining to Sean and me that we should be extra kind to the new girl next door because she didn't have a mother or a father and was living with her grandmother. I don't think I ever asked you about it a single time growing up. It seemed taboo."

Destiny shrugged. "I don't know much."

"I don't mean to make you sad. We don't have to talk about it if you don't want to. I was just curious."

Destiny shook her head. "It doesn't make me sad.

Not anymore. I really can't complain. I was so very lucky. My grandmother wanted me more than anything, and she's never once acted like I was a burden to her. She loves me enough for ten parents."

Trent smiled. "She does."

"And so does *your* mother. I guess she felt sorry for me or whatever, but I'll never forget her kindness when I was young and scared and living in a strange house with a grandmother I never knew existed."

Trent nodded as he chewed another bite. "I always thought you filled something in my mom. She never had a daughter, and you gave her a piece of that."

Destiny's chest tightened. She loved Trent's mom as much as any child could love their own mother. "I'm glad we had each other."

"Do you remember your mom? You were five at the time."

Destiny tipped her head to one side. "Honestly, not very well. I remember we lived in this trailer home and it was filthy. She slept a lot. She was too skinny and didn't shower and rarely cooked. Most of the time, I think she forgot about me."

Trent set his fork down. "Jesus, Des. I'm so sorry. That must have been hard."

"I didn't know any different."

"What about your dad?"

"Never met him. Or I don't remember it. I just remember that one day my mom left and never came back. I ate out of a box of cereal for an entire day before I went next door to the neighbor's and asked the older woman who lived there if she knew where my mommy was. She called the police. I remember the squad car because it had flashing blue lights and I got to ride in it. I spent a few nights with a foster family, though I didn't understand that at the time. And then the authorities located my grandmother and she came and got me."

"Wow. I feel bad that I never asked you that story."

"It's no big deal. I mean, I'm a grown adult. I had a great life. I assume my mother got pregnant and never told my father or didn't know who he was. Much later, when I was older, my grandmother told me the trailer had been filled with drug paraphernalia. I assume my mother OD'd somewhere without identification on her. Her purse was still in the trailer."

"That sucks. The not knowing."

"Yeah. For a few years, my grandma tried to find her, and my father, but it took a lot of time and money, and eventually she gave up. The police weren't very interested in searching for a drug addict."

Trent stared at her for a long time.

Finally, Destiny shook off the melancholy and smiled at him. "It's done. It's in the past. I've made peace with it. I had my grandma and your parents. I had two amazing friends next door. I wanted for nothing."

"If you want, I could try to track her down. DNA is easier to trace nowadays. I could give a lock of your hair to a guy I know and see if it matches anything in the database. If she by chance died and was never identified, we might get a match. Who knows? We might even be able to find your father."

Destiny chewed on her bottom lip. "Maybe. I don't know. Sometimes I wish I knew, just so I can stop wondering. I bet my grandma would rest easier if she knew about her daughter, too. What if you don't get a match? Would that mean she might still be alive?"

Trent shrugged. "It's a possibility."

"That might be worse. Knowing she's dead could help me and my grandma have closure, but if there's no match… That could just make us worry and wonder even more. I'm afraid I might actually feel angry with my mom if she's alive out there and never once tried to find me."

"I can understand that. Keep in mind, if your mom was a drug addict, chances are not good she's still alive after all these years. That's hard to swallow also."

Destiny sighed. This subject was too heavy. They needed to talk about something else. "New topic. Let's discuss something more uplifting." She forced a smile.

Trent reached over and covered her hand with his. "Excellent plan. Let's toss the dishes in the sink and move to the living room."

She liked this idea. She liked everything about this second date of theirs. It was so…domestic. She had no idea Trent could cook. She wanted to know everything about him. He'd changed since high school. Not to say that his personality was different. It wasn't. But he'd added experiences, likes and dislikes. She wanted to hear all of them and tell him hers.

And that's exactly what they did. For the next three hours, they sat on his couch, laughing about memories from when they were kids and adding to the list of life experiences they'd had since high school.

Between the two of them, they had traveled all over

the world, so they compared the places they'd been and discussed mutual places they wanted to visit. Trent never stopped touching her. He either held her hand, or when she needed both hands to tell an animated story, he set his palm on her shoulder or thigh or neck.

She noticed every touch, every stroke of his fingers, the way he held her gaze while she spoke, the way he licked his lips when he watched hers, the way he leaned into her often. It was so comfortable. Like time hadn't passed. They'd been like this when they were younger. Carefree and easygoing together.

Trent had been the more comical of the brothers. The relationship she'd had with him was filled with jokes and teasing and humor. In contrast, when she'd been alone with Sean, they'd discussed more serious things. Sean had been more introspective, wondering how things worked and why. He'd been more cautious. A rule follower.

When Destiny was a kid, she'd needed both influences. Both boys had shaped her and nurtured her differently. When she'd been sad, Sean would notice and hug her. Trent would notice too, but he would make her laugh. The balance between them was perfect until Sean ruptured it by asking her out.

Looking back, she recognized the signs. While she had thought Trent pushed her away, he'd really done so out of self-preservation. She should've known something wasn't right when he stopped joking with her and grew more serious and withdrawn. Perhaps she'd been unable to focus on Trent's reaction because she was so focused on her own mistakes and the fact that she was slowly sliding down a long embankment, feeling like there was no way to climb back out.

As she stared at Trent now, she forced herself not to dwell on lost time. They were adults now. Maybe they couldn't have made things work before their maturity had shaped them. They would never know, but there was no going back. All she could do was be grateful she'd gotten drunk and dumped more than a decade of frustration at his feet.

They'd been silent for several moments now, talked out, simply enjoying each other's company. She felt happier than she had in a long time, and that expression was reflected back to her on his face.

"Des..." His voice was deep, serious.

She licked her lips.

His gaze shifted to her mouth. "I'm going to kiss you, and then you're going to go home."

She sighed, nodding slowly. She didn't want to leave. She didn't want this to end. She wanted to stay all night, find out what it would be like to really be with him in every sense.

He groaned. "Don't look at me like that. I'm trying to be a gentleman."

"I didn't ask you to be a gentleman," she pointed out.

"I'm doing it anyway. I've had the best time tonight. I did on our last date, too. I want you more than I've ever wanted a woman before. That's why you're going to leave, and I'm going to keep my pants on."

She scrunched up her face. "Does that make sense?"

"Yep. It's respectful, and I want things between us to be perfect the first time we have sex. So, we're going to wait. I don't want to be in the middle of a mission that's hanging over me. I want to be fully present. I want you to know that for whatever time we are together, you're number one. Right now, I can't do that. I need to get on the phone with my team and get updated on the last few hours."

"I understand." She did. Although he hadn't mentioned his current strange local mission a single time in the last few hours, obviously it hadn't gone away. She was grateful he'd taken the time to make sure she knew he was in this with her. "Thank you for tonight."

He stood, took her hand, and tugged her to her feet. Next, he cupped her face and closed the distance. His kiss started tender and slow, nibbling, tasting, teasing. And then he pulled her more fully against him, threaded his fingers in her hair at the back of her head, and deepened the contact.

She moaned as his tongue swept against hers, her mind spinning. It felt so damn good when he held her like this, taking control. All rational thought left just as it had the other times he'd kissed her. It was as if he poured his soul into the kiss. She felt it deeply and craved more.

As far as Destiny was concerned, his unwillingness to have sex with her fueled her desire to be naked with him more than if he'd dragged her into his bedroom.

She ran her hands down his back and lower still until she cupped his ass, squeezing it and pulling him against her. His erection pressed into her belly.

He moaned into her mouth and let one hand slide

down to cup her breast. The moment he squeezed, she arched into him, her body on fire. Her nipple stabbed at the lace of her bra as he flicked his thumb over it.

"Des…" he murmured against her lips.

She whimpered. "Please. Trent…" She wasn't too proud not to beg. She wanted this man. She'd wanted him half her life. Now that she'd had a taste of him, she had no interest in waiting. Life was short.

His hand roamed down her belly and two seconds later, he popped the button and lowered the zipper. *Thank God.*

Eager to take things to the next level, she reached between them to cup his cock.

He grabbed her wrist and pulled her hand behind her back.

While she blinked at him, he wrestled her other hand to join the first and then clasped one of his hands around both wrists.

She gasped, her body even more alert than it had been a moment ago. Something about the way he restrained her made her even hornier. And then he met and held her gaze as he backed her up until her butt hit the padded arm of a chair.

"Don't move." His voice was deep, gravelly.

She sucked in a breath.

When he flattened his hand on her belly and slid it down into her panties, she whimpered. "If you stay perfectly still, I'll make you come, Des. Can you do that?"

Can I do that? Fuck yes. Who would turn down an offer like that? Besides, the dirty talk alone drove her to the edge. She'd rather reciprocate, but she wouldn't complain. If the man had some reason why he didn't want to have sex with her tonight, fine. But he could at least accept a blowjob.

That thought fled her mind the moment his fingers found her clit. Two seconds later, her knees were shaking, and she was glad for the armchair behind her butt to keep her upright.

She gasped, her mouth falling open when he thrust two fingers into her. His palm ground against her clit. Before she could wrap her mind around what was happening, he added a third finger, and she stopped thinking altogether.

He thrust them in and out of her, his palm repeatedly grinding against her swollen nub. When he leaned in closer and set his lips on her ear, she shivered.

And then he whispered, "Come, Des. Come on my fingers. I want to feel your pussy pulsing around my hand."

That was all it took. She crashed over the edge, shuddering as her body obeyed him. Her orgasm took her by surprise and left her panting as it slowly subsided.

When Trent finally eased his hand out of her pants and lifted it to his mouth to suck her arousal from his fingers, she moaned. "Jesus, Trent."

He still held her wrists behind her.

"Can I at least reciprocate?" she whimpered.

"Nope." He smiled at her. "Not tonight. Another time."

She took several deep breaths while she marveled at

how damn lucky she was to have found Trent again after all these years. He was back in her life. He might be dragging his feet over some concerns about his current mission, but after that orgasm, she felt confident he wasn't humoring her. At least she wouldn't go to bed at night wondering if he cared.

When he finally released her wrists, he cupped her face again and kissed her deeply. He was breathing heavily by the time he broke free. "You have no idea how badly I want to take you to bed instead of sending you back to your grandmother's."

"Trent..." Would it do any good to point out she was a willing participant in this plan?

He shook his head. "I need to concentrate on my job right now, Des. I swear, when this is over..."

"Okay." She definitely didn't want to mess with his mojo while he was on an assignment.

He reached down to tug her jeans back into place, and she batted his hands away to zip and button them.

Without another word, he grabbed her hand and led her toward the door.

She snagged her purse off his coffee table on the way.

At the door, he faced her again, his hands cupping her neck, his thumbs stroking her cheeks. "I need you to do something for me."

"Anything."

"Don't come here again. Not while I'm on this mission. Please trust me, Des. My hands are tied. I'll make every effort to see you as often as I can, but you need to wait for me to contact you. I know that's a lot to ask, but I have no choice. When I can break free, I'll tell you where to meet me. I'll pick someplace between Dallas and Killeen on a day you're off. Okay?"

She chuckled. "It seems like the tables have turned. I should be elated. After all, I told you I didn't want anyone to know we were dating. If we sneak around in another town, no one will find out about us. I'm getting what I wanted, aren't I?" *Why does it feel so...off...so wrong?*

He didn't smile back. Instead, his brows drew together. His lips parted and closed a few times as if he wasn't sure what he wanted to say. Finally, he cleared his throat. "Des... When I'm done with this mission, if you're still willing to date someone like me, then we'll readdress this arrangement. In the meantime, I guess you're getting what you wanted. I promise no one will find out we're dating." His fingers stiffened on her neck as if his words didn't quite match his thoughts.

She stared into his eyes, deciding to hold her tongue. She couldn't imagine what he wasn't telling her, but she had only two choices—trust that he had his reasons for being so evasive, probably job-related, or walk away and never look back. Option two wasn't an option at all, so for now, she was going to have to trust him. "Okay."

He gave her a slight smile and kissed her one last time. "Be careful driving, and tell your grandmother I said hello."

"I will." Her heart beat rapidly as he opened the door and slowly released her hand.

She held her breath, fighting an emotional avalanche as she made her way to her car. She held it together until she was inside with the door shut, and then she blew out a breath. A tear escaped and she wiped it away. There was no reason for her to feel so damn unnerved. Trent hadn't said anything that should alarm her.

Except he had. Maybe not his words, but his tone. They'd had an amazing evening together, and then her fun-loving Trent had gotten all serious and basically told her, "Don't call me. I'll call you." Maybe it was best that they hadn't slept together. If they had, his next call would have seemed like a booty call. Destiny wanted much more than that, and she hoped Trent still did, too. Something definitely felt off.

CHAPTER 16

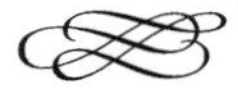

The moment Trent shut his door, he texted Merlin.

She just left.

I'm on it.

Can't thank you enough.

No thanks needed, Zip. You know that. We're a team.

Trent knew that well. He would do anything for his teammates, and they would likewise do anything for him, even if this time it meant following his woman back to her grandmother's house to keep her safe.

Trent busied himself cleaning his kitchen and then sat at the kitchen table with his laptop. This entire situation was a fucking mess. He'd just lied to Destiny, and she knew it. His omissions were obvious to her. Her mistrust was in her eyes even though she hadn't said a word.

When he thought back on everything he'd said, he groaned. He wouldn't go out with himself again after hearing that ridiculous speech.

"Don't call me."

"Don't come to my apartment."

"I'll let you know when I can see you."

"We'll meet in secret locations so no one finds out about us."

Jesus. If Destiny didn't know him better or wasn't committed to making this work, she'd have to assume he was either embarrassed to be seen with her, married, or a serial killer.

He ran a hand through his hair, set his elbows on the table, and closed his eyes. He was a selfish prick for dragging her down this path with him. Why he'd ever thought it would be a good idea to bring a woman into his life was beyond him. He'd never even considered entering into a serious relationship. His job meant he would disappear on a moment's notice and be gone for long periods of time with no contact.

And all that was before he'd added the unforeseen aspect of someone hunting him down on U.S. soil with the intent to kill him. At least until this mission, Trent had always lived in the relative comfort of believing when he was home, he was free. Now, that notion had exploded.

Even if he somehow managed to locate and eliminate this threat, there would simply be another right behind it. Best case scenario at the moment was for Trent's team to locate Farid Demir and take him into custody or end his life. *Then what?* That would never be the end. Onur would lose his shit if his brother didn't return home having accomplished his mission. Onur would send someone else.

Trent's entire team as well as Commander Turano were well aware of this problem. It was unspoken but filled every meeting room with its ominousness. Roe's furrowed brow when they met spoke volumes. Trent was fucked, and no one had thought of a way out of this mess.

He had no business dragging a civilian into his problems. Not his mom, his dad, or Destiny. Every time he saw her, he would be putting her at risk. Was it worth it? After all, Trent was a ticking time bomb. His days seemed to be numbered. Maybe he could evade Farid for a few more weeks. Maybe his team would find the fucker and take him out. But then what? They sat around waiting for Onur to send his next hitman?

In no scenario could Trent fathom life after this threat. It didn't exist. He had no business spending time with Destiny. It simply made things harder. He was selfish and greedy for even considering it or giving her hope that he would call and set something clandestine up with her.

He felt like a world-class fuck for acting like he was doing this for her. What a joke. He hadn't believed for a moment that the town or his parents would flinch to find out Trent was dating Destiny, but *she* did. She'd shared how people talked behind her back, and that killed him because he hadn't known when he should have. As for those who did that, fuck them. He didn't care what they thought, so long as they kept their opinions to themselves and left Destiny alone.

Granted, out of respect for Destiny's feelings and because he had never walked in her shoes, he would grant her anything she wanted. But the truth was, he'd taken her request and twisted it into this giant lie. He did so to protect himself, but when she found out—and she would—she would be so damn furious with him, she would probably walk away anyway.

What a fucking disaster.

Trent shoved from the table and stomped to his bedroom. There was no way he could concentrate on research right now. His head was in the wrong place. He needed to change into workout clothes and make use of his limited weights and treadmill to work himself hard and drive himself to exhaustion. Only then could he manage to sleep.

CHAPTER 17

"Talk to me, Zip."

Trent was pacing his apartment, which he'd been doing for hours. Woof had arrived fifteen minutes ago and was sitting on the sofa, elbows on his knees, hands rubbing together. He knew as well as Trent this current situation was a shitshow.

When Trent first moved into this apartment, he'd been rather fond of it. The layout seemed good. The view. The kitchen was larger than average. It was freshly painted and had newer carpet. Now? Now, he never wanted to see it again.

"What do you want to know?" he asked Woof.

"I get that you're stir-crazy, but I've never seen you this frustrated. You're usually the most upbeat one of all of us."

Trent rolled his eyes. "You come here where I'm basically in hiding, where I spent several hours with my woman last night, and tell me that Demir has fucking been spotted in Dallas, and you want me to fucking calm down? Jesus, Destiny lives in Dallas."

Woof nodded. "You're right. I get it. It's fucked up. We can keep an eye on Destiny's place if it'll make you feel better."

"Is there any chance they're wrong? Maybe the guy they've tagged is someone else?" Trent was grasping at straws here. His team didn't make mistakes, and no way would Woof come over and lower this kind of boom on him if he hadn't triple-checked the details himself.

"Roe is emailing you the surveillance pics. Trust me. It's him. First a gas station and then a motel."

Trent stopped pacing to look out the window, seeing nothing.

Behind him, Woof took a deep breath and blew it out. "Speaking of, how'd it go last night with Destiny?" Trent appreciated that Woof would do anything to keep Trent's mind off the danger he was in.

Trent sighed. "Fantastic. And I need to stop seeing her."

"Why would you do that?"

He spun around and leaned against the window sill. "I could ask you how you manage a long-distance relationship with Nori. I could ask you how you juggle your job and hers. I could ask for advice on how to make this work. But the truth is, none of that matters in my case. I'll never be a free man. I'm dragging her into a dangerous situation every time I see her. Putting her life at great risk. And now you tell me Farid is fucking stalking me."

"We don't know that yet. There's no evidence he's found you. He just knows where we're all stationed."

Trent rolled his eyes. "Great. I feel so much better."

Woof leaned forward. "Forget Farid for a moment. About Destiny. You can't think like that. We all know what the commitment is to Delta Force, and yet many of us have managed to meet a significant other who's willing to put up with our weird hours and crappy availability. Not just any woman can make that commitment. It takes a special person with immeasurable strength to overlook our inability to discuss a mission, the constant secrets, the sudden calls to duty. But women like that exist. Nori is one of them. Hell, she's working overseas. We're both making a sacrifice."

Trent pulled in a long breath. "I might have seen your point until this shit happened. What no one on the team is willing to say out loud even though all of us know it's true, is that I'll never be safe again. Demir won't give up. We can capture his brother and lock him up, but Demir will just send another hitman. You know it. We all know it. I don't want Destiny to know it, however. It's not fair to her."

"First of all, we're going to work our asses off to put an end to this threat, so don't talk like it's not possible to squelch it for good. We're a team. We've got this. We've handled worse missions than this in the past and won. We will this time, too."

Trent had lost the ability to believe that was even an option, so he didn't respond.

"Second of all, you don't get to make decisions for Destiny. All you can do is give her the facts and let her decide what she is willing to live with."

Trent jerked his face up to respond. "You know I can't talk to her about this mission or any other. My hands are tied. And she left here last night looking at me with mistrust. I've given her no reason to trust me at all on every occasion we've gotten together. Why should she? I've been lying to her, and I keep insisting we sneak around so no one knows we're seeing each other. It's crazy. I have no idea why she would ever take another call from me again."

Woof shook his head. "I'm not suggesting you mention the specifics. I'm saying you should tell her you're in danger. Give her just enough so that she will understand the gravity of this situation. If you at least explain why you're not available to go to dinner and a movie, she won't have to be so suspicious."

Trent's shoulders dropped. "Not going to happen."

"Why the hell not?"

"Because I don't want her to worry. She already lost my brother to an IED. I won't have her thinking some sharpshooter might take me out while we're walking to the car. She'd never be able to deal with the loss of yet another boyfriend serving his country."

Woof sighed. "Like I said before, you can't make that decision for her."

"I already did. I don't want her to worry. I don't want her life in danger, either. And I sure as fuck don't want that problem to follow her around for the rest of her life. She's better off without me. She should find a nice man who isn't wanted by a guerilla group in Kazarus."

Trent turned back to face the window. He didn't want to argue this point anymore. He was exhausted from not getting enough sleep. He really needed to make a clean break with Destiny and get his head screwed back on straight before his distraction got him shot in the head.

When Woof spoke again, he was standing much closer. "I can practically see you digging your heels in on this. Stop it. Don't put your life on hold. We've all got your back. Make another plan with her. Why don't you meet her in Lancelot or something? It's a small town. Off the beaten path. We'll make sure you aren't detected leaving town, and we'll have your back."

Trent smirked. "Lancelot. What the fuck's in Lancelot? Did you pull that out of your ass?"

Woof chuckled. "It was the first thing that came to mind. It's a small town with an amazing bookstore called Camelot Rare Books and Antiquities. Meet her there. She'll probably love the place. I haven't met anyone who didn't."

Trent stared at Woof for several seconds. "I don't know. Feels like I'm postponing the inevitable and leading Destiny down a dead-end road. It's not fair to her."

"Look, I know you two have history and all, so you already knew each other when you hooked up that night at the bar—"

Trent interrupted. "'Hooked up' is a pretty strong term for me carrying a very drunk Destiny back to my apartment to vomit and sleep off her hangover. It's not like we slept together."

Woof shrugged. "Whatever. Not important. The point is that you've been on two amazing dates since then. I'm going to assume they went very well or you wouldn't be so torn and out of sorts. We're in a holding pattern here until Farid Demir makes himself visible again. At least we've got him pinned down to a city. In the meantime, go after the woman who has you tied in knots. Don't let her slip away without making certain. If she's the one, none of this will matter. You'll find a way to make it work."

Trent swallowed over the lump in his throat. "I don't need another date with Destiny to know if she's the one. I didn't even need the first date. I was certain in my heart the morning she woke up in my apartment all tousled and hungover. If I'm honest with myself, I knew I'd struck gold from the moment she started blabbering all drunk and cute in that bar, telling me how she'd felt about me her entire life. I'm pretty sure I was done for that very second."

Woof smiled. "Then stop acting like a fool and make another plan. Don't let her slip away over this shit. You know you have four teammates who will absolutely take out this threat even if we all die trying."

Trent knew Woof was right about that last part. He would do anything for his team. They had a bond. They had each other's backs. Nothing would ever break that kind of camaraderie and commitment. "Fine, but if you're gonna be so damn invested in making sure I have a woman in my life, you better have my six."

"You know it, brother. Always."

CHAPTER 18

Destiny smiled as the chime sounded over the doorway when she stepped into the quaint bookstore in Lancelot, Texas. Camelot Rare Books & Antiquities. The smell of old books made her close her eyes and inhale slowly. It was late afternoon, and she knew she was early, but it didn't matter. She could easily spend hours in this bookstore.

"Good afternoon," came a voice from behind the register. "Can I help you find anything?"

Destiny turned her gaze to the young woman behind the counter and headed her direction. "I'm actually meeting someone here. He thought this would be a good location in case he was late." Destiny glanced around at the treasure trove of antiques and old books. "He was obviously right. What a cute store. I've heard about this place for years, but I've never stopped in Lancelot to explore."

The woman smiled as she rounded the counter and held out a hand. "I'm Gwen. I'll have to thank him for the recommendation." Gwen had gorgeous red hair that didn't want to stay tucked behind her ears.

"Even if Trent doesn't show up for hours, I won't be disappointed. Who wouldn't enjoy getting stuck in a treasure trove of old books?"

"I agree. I could stay in here for days or years. Oh wait, that's exactly what I do," she joked.

Destiny laughed. "There's no way I can keep from asking how on earth a woman named Gwen owns a bookstore named Camelot in a town called Lancelot."

Gwen smiled. "It's over the top, isn't it?" She took a breath. "Simple really. My grandparents and parents are obsessed with Arthurian legend. So, they named me Guinevere." She shrugged.

"I don't suppose you're married to a man named Arthur?" Destiny teased.

"Nope. Not married at all. But that's my dad's name."

Destiny chuckled. "Of course it is. I do know a man named Merlin."

Gwen's cute freckles danced on her cheeks as she smiled. "Can't say I've ever met a Merlin."

"He's a friend of Trent's."

"And Trent is your boyfriend?"

"I'm not sure I'm ready to call him my boyfriend yet, but maybe."

Gwen grinned. "He must be a romantic if he asked you to meet him here at Camelot."

Destiny shrugged. "Can't tell you that yet, either. Jury is still out. We actually just reconnected after not seeing each other for many years. We've only really seen each other three times this month. The first one hardly counts since I was drunk."

Gwen's eyes widened. "You got drunk on your first date?"

"Nope. I ran into him at a bar one night and drained several tequila shots so I could find the courage to blab my lifelong lust for him like a crazy woman."

Gwen's face lit up further. "I love it. So now what? Why are you meeting him in Lancelot?"

Destiny shrugged. "Trent is in the Army. He's in the middle of some sort of local mission and he refuses to meet up with me any place where someone might see us." Destiny glanced around again. There weren't any other customers in the store right now, but she felt bad monopolizing Gwen's time. "Sorry. I'm talking your ear off. I'm sure you have other things you'd rather be doing."

Gwen shook her head and waved a hand through the air. "Not at all. Meeting interesting people is my favorite part of this job. Well, okay, next to finding a first edition of *Walden*. Your story is fascinating. You think Trent is protecting you?"

Destiny sighed. "I don't know. Maybe. I'm trying not to be 'that woman,' the mistrustful kind who nags and whines, but it's been a challenge."

"I'm sure you're not. You don't seem like that to me at all." Gwen leaned back against the counter.

"Yeah, well, the irony is that I'm the one who insisted we take things slow and keep our relationship secretive. I've known his parents most of my life and didn't want them to find out about us just in case we decided we didn't have a spark. And I didn't want the town to know prematurely so the gossip mills wouldn't start up. I was insistent. And then my idea began to seem absurd after our first date. I couldn't even remember why the hell I would care if anyone knew we were dating. Suddenly, the tables turned and it's Trent who insists we sneak around. He's gone out of his way this time to meet me out of town and hide from anyone we might know."

Gwen just nodded slowly, waiting for more.

"Honestly, I'm starting to wonder if he's embarrassed to be seen with me. He originally thought I'd lost my mind, but then he switched sides and agreed we should hide. Now, it's grown absurd. If I was waiting for clarity about my feelings for him, I had that in spades about ten minutes into our first date. Now, I'd rather go straight to his parents and spill the entire secret. But nooo… I'm in Lancelot, thirty minutes from Killeen, meeting Trent for a clandestine rendezvous." Destiny heard the sarcasm in her voice and winced. "Sorry, that was totally TMI."

Gwen looked skeptical. "I've never met Trent of course, but if he's working this hard to see you, surely he has a good reason for his odd secrecy."

Destiny nodded. "Maybe you're right." Destiny felt a weight lift from this conversation. She liked Gwen, and the woman was a great listener.

When the chime over the front door sounded, Destiny turned her head to find Trent strolling into the bookstore, alert for any signs of her. Destiny's heartbeat picked up. Yeah, she was in so much trouble. She wasn't just falling for him—she *had* fallen, hard. She needed to suck up her concerns, give him the benefit of the doubt, and go on the best third date of her life.

She just prayed that this time, they ended up in bed. She wanted to show off some of her skills. Besides, her vibrator had been taking a beating lately.

CHAPTER 19

"You seem happy," Trent pointed out over dinner. "Your face is lit up more than the last few times I saw you." He was holding her hand across the table like he had been since they sat down, releasing her only occasionally so they could take a few bites and get a drink.

She shrugged. "I am happy. Shouldn't I be? After all, I have two days off and I managed to land a date with the hottest man in Texas who happened to be available when I am. I'm pretty sure I frightened Libby with my squeal when you called to suggest this."

He smiled. "Good. I'm glad. I feel bad about you driving all the way to Lancelot and then back here to the outskirts of Killeen. I hope you don't mind that I booked us a room without asking first. I don't want you to take it to mean we have to have sex or anything. I just want to spend as much time with you as possible." They had dropped her car off in the hotel parking lot about thirty minutes from Killeen before heading to dinner, and she hadn't said a word in protest.

She took a sip of her wine and set the glass down slowly, meeting Trent's gaze head-on. "Trent, I'm ecstatic that you got us a hotel room, and I will only be pissed if you don't lose the chivalry this time. Enough foreplay. I'm done waiting."

One corner of his mouth lifted in a wry grin. "You sure? I don't ever want you to think I rushed you."

"*Rushed* me? Jesus, Trent. I've known you twenty-five years. You know more about me than anyone alive. I hardly think us sleeping together at this stage is rushed."

Trent inhaled slowly, holding her gaze, and then he jerked his head toward the waitress and lifted his hand. The only thing missing was a cliché *check please.*

Destiny giggled. It was hard to sit still. She wanted to get to the good part. Now. Every inch of her body wanted to be naked against him, learning every contour of his rock-hard frame. She wanted his hands on her bare skin, stroking, teasing, tormenting. She wanted him *now.*

It took an eon for the waitress to bring the check and Trent to pay the bill. He walked her to the car at a leisurely pace as if he hadn't just heard her suggest they round the damn bases immediately.

He might have driven over the speed limit, however, though he did that without any jerky movements that gave away a sense of urgency. He checked them into their room just as casually.

By the time they reached the door, she was nervous, thinking she'd been too forward and deciding he wasn't as eager.

And that was her last coherent thought.

The moment the door shut, he dropped their bags and she found herself plastered to the back of the door. One second, they were strolling casually down the hallway. The next, her ass hit the door and the breath whooshed from her lungs. He tugged the band out of her hair and threaded his fingers in it as he lowered his lips to hers.

Her heart was racing from the sudden change, but she smiled against his lips and quickly melted as he claimed her mouth. His body pressed into hers as his knee came between her thighs. His hands were everywhere, exploring up and down her body as if he only had moments to memorize her, and then his exploration would have to last him a lifetime.

Destiny moaned when he palmed her breasts. She arched her chest, loving this dominant side of him. Every inch of her was already on fire. She'd been aroused from the moment he picked her up at the bookstore. That need had grown incrementally during dinner.

When his hands slid down to reach under her shirt, she whimpered, blinking in the dim light in the room. Apparently, housekeeping had left a single small lamp turned on next to the bed.

He finally broke the kiss long enough to meet her gaze. His voice was gravelly and low and serious. "Remember that romantic guy who held you all night and made you come against his hand with your jeans on?"

"Yeah," she breathed as a shiver raced up her spine.

"Remember the one who clasped your wrists behind your back and slid his hand down your jeans on our second date?"

"Yes." That word came out even breathier.

"Well, that second guy is here tonight. He's the alter ego of the first guy. He's a bit more demanding. Want to get to know him better?" Trent's expression remained sober. His words were almost funny, but he meant them to be serious.

Destiny slowly smiled. "I'd be delighted." Her body shuddered as she considered his meaning. She didn't have long to think about it though because Trent had her shirt over her head and was unclasping her bra before she took her next breath. He yanked his shirt off next and then cupped her breasts again, his rough skin against her sensitive flesh.

Trent's gaze came to hers as he pinched both her nipples and twisted them.

She rose onto her tiptoes as she gasped. The slight pain sent a wave of arousal to her pussy. "Trent…"

"Yeah, that's the tone I want you to use when you say my name."

She couldn't respond because all her concentration was on the way he plucked her nipples until they were tight and swollen. She willed him to suck on them, and moments later, she got her wish when his head descended and he drew one tight bud into his mouth.

Destiny cried out at the intensity of the contact, a strange pleasure/pain rushing through her body.

His free hand reached between her legs to cup her pussy with so much force that he nearly lifted her off the floor. And then, with her nipple still in his mouth, he went to work on her jeans, unfastening them and tugging them down while she could do little more than grab his biceps, knowing this wild ride was going to be her undoing.

Destiny had had sex over the years. She'd dated guys, sometimes even for a few months. But nothing, absolutely nothing, in her sexual repertoire compared to what she was experiencing right now. Hell, nothing came close to what Trent had done to her last week, either. Fully clothed.

But this... God, this was so much more. Her arousal was through the roof. Urgency caused her to reach for the button on his jeans.

His mouth released her nipple, but only long enough to clasp on to the other bud. He flicked his tongue over the tip rapidly, making her knees weak. It was impossible to undo his button because few messages were making it to her hands.

Trent was grinning when he released her second nipple and met her gaze. He batted her hands away and removed his jeans. "Scale of one to ten, how ready are you for me?"

She licked her lips, shuddering again. "Twelve."

He smiled wider and reached between her legs, two fingers finding her folds, spreading them, and thrusting into her.

Destiny cried out.

"Yeah, that's what I thought."

She moaned as he continued to thrust in and out of her, his fingers curling toward the front of her channel. He never took his gaze off hers. When his thumb landed on her clit and pressed against her sensitive flesh, she grabbed his biceps again. "Trent…" She was going to come embarrassingly quickly yet again.

"That's it. That's the voice I love. Say my name again while I make you come."

Her head rolled backward. She'd never come standing against a wall. She wouldn't have even though it was possible. But here she was. So close. Desperate. Greedy. Hornier than she'd ever been in her life.

"Now, Des. Come for me."

Her pussy clenched down on his fingers as the pulses of her orgasm washed through her.

"That's it. That's my girl. So damn sexy. I'll never get enough of watching you come, Des."

She moaned unabashedly through the orgasm, for the first time in her life feeling completely at ease with a man. This was Trent. No way would she hold back or permit herself to be embarrassed with him.

Shocking herself, instead of collapsing against him in a sated pile of putty, she wanted more, and now that she'd come so thoroughly against his hand, she was energized. She slid both hands to his hips and then reached between their two bodies to wrap her palm around his long, thick length.

When he lowered his gaze to their connection, she did the same. His cock was thick and hard, the tip a deep red with the evidence of his arousal leaking from the slit. One second she was staring in fascination as she eased her hand up and down his shaft. The next second, she was on her knees in front of him, eagerly flicking her tongue over the pearl of come on his tip.

Trent leaned forward, his hands landing flat against the door, making a smacking noise that reverberated through the room. "Des..."

The way he murmured her name emboldened her. She slid her mouth over his erection, drawing it in deep.

Damn, he was thick. He was going to stretch her deliciously when he slid into her pussy. Of course, it didn't hurt that it had been a while since she'd last been with a man.

Drawing her tongue up his shaft as she slid almost off, she inhaled his scent and learned his flavor. Salty. Musky. Trent. She'd visualized this intimate connection with him thousands of times, and here she was.

She sucked him deeper on the next pass as he moaned and leaned into her.

Suddenly, he gasped and pulled out of her mouth. "Jesus, Des." He grabbed her biceps and urged her to stand. His mouth was on hers again before she could take a breath, devouring her. His cock bobbed against her stomach while he urgently kissed her as if his life depended on it.

When he broke free, he bent down and grabbed his jeans. A second later, he was rolling a condom on his erection. His gaze came to hers again. "I need to be inside you."

She nodded. "Please, Trent." She felt the same urgency, like she wouldn't be able to stop squirming until he took her. For a moment, she was certain he would take her against the wall, but then he grabbed her by the waist, spun her around, and set her ass on the edge of the nearest surface—the desk. There was a bed less than a few feet behind him, but he didn't bother to check.

He cupped her face with one hand and dragged the tip of his erection through her slit with the other. "I can't hold back."

"I don't want you to." She held his gaze as she smoothed her hands up his biceps and then around his neck. She wrapped her legs around his hips and arched into him, urging him to enter her. Every nerve ending in her body was alight, pleading for this connection. She'd wanted this nearly half her life, and here she was, in Trent's arms, his eyes on hers, his cock at her entrance, an expression of reverence on his face.

"Des..." He thrust into her as he called her name.

She gasped, her mouth falling open. So full. So tight. So perfect.

For a long time, he held himself steady deep inside her, both of them breathing heavily as if they'd run hard to get to this mountain peak and needed to pause and savor the view. And the view was amazing. He held her gaze, his mouth curved up in a smile.

Finally, he blew out a deep breath and took her lips again. The shared moment of awe was broken as he drew almost out and thrust back into her.

She whimpered against his lips, her body more alive than it had ever been. This was nothing like the other guys she'd dated or hooked up with. This was Trent. He owned a piece of her, and he was claiming it now.

Energy sizzled around them as they moved together

over and over, urgency in the air. It felt so good, having him this close, inside her, filling her.

Trent's hands roamed everywhere, gripping her breasts and then her back and then finally settling on her ass to hold her close to the edge of the table. Every move had a sense of desperation that she felt just as strongly.

She slid her hands to his shoulder blades and dug her fingertips into his muscles, arching her hips forward to increase the contact between her clit and the base of his cock. She'd never come from penetration alone before, but she was so close…

Trent released her lips and set his forehead against hers. "Des… My God." He never stopped thrusting, but he shifted one hand around between their bodies and found the swollen bundle of nerves that was about to explode. "Come around my cock, Des. I want to feel you before I let go."

She tipped her head back and moaned, concentrating on his fingers as they circled and then stroked her clit while his erection continued to fill her over and over. The pressure increased, the tension growing higher until she couldn't hold back. Her entire body stiffened when she reached the edge.

Trent pressed a finger hard against her clit, pushing her over the edge. "That's my girl. So. Gorgeous. I'll never. Tire. Of watching. You come." Each word chopped. Separated. Gravelly. Each one punctuated by another thrust.

She shuddered as the pulses consumed her until Trent held himself deep and groaned out his release.

The sound filled her, burrowing under her skin. She would never forget the tone of his release and how expressive he was as he came.

Finally, both of them spent and gasping for oxygen, Trent managed to lift her off the desk with both hands under her butt. “Hold on, Des.”

She wrapped her arms and legs around him tight as he carried her to the bed. His still-erect shaft remained inside her, and she paid no attention to anything but his blissful expression as he lowered them onto the bed.

Yeah, date three was definitely a hit. She was shattered.

CHAPTER 20

"Des..." Trent smoothed her hair away from her face and kissed her cheek. It was early, but he couldn't stay in bed with her all day. He needed to get back to base in a few hours. Roe had called a team meeting for late morning.

Trent nibbled a path down Destiny's neck and lower until he could flick his tongue over her nipple. He wanted to spend some time talking to her before he had to leave. He had something he needed to tell her. It was time.

She finally whimpered softly, her hand sliding up his arm. "What time is it?" she whispered.

"Early." He hated this. Hated it with a passion. He wanted to stay here in bed with her for the rest of his life. But he didn't have that luxury. Not right now. Not with Demir lurking around somewhere watching Trent's every move. Waiting for his opportunity.

After making love to Destiny two more times until

neither of them had the energy to think, Trent had set an alarm and then watched her sleep.

Damn, she was sexy. Every inch of her. Her lithe body fit perfectly against him. Long toned legs, pert breasts, rich, smooth skin. He'd been mesmerized by her from the day they met when they were five years old.

He would never tire of staring at her. He wouldn't have to imagine the color of her nipples anymore, he could easily visualize their dark hue when he closed his eyes and took himself in hand. There was little doubt that was going to happen often now that he'd had her but couldn't be with her frequently.

She rolled into him, her arm wrapping around his middle. "So sleepy…"

He pulled her close against him and kissed her temple, his hand threading into her hair. "You smell so good."

She giggled, coming more awake. "Not sure how that's possible."

"Mmm. It must be your shampoo or body wash. I remember it from when we were younger. Vanilla. You haven't changed it."

She tipped her head back to meet his gaze. "How the hell can you remember that?"

He shrugged. "It's embedded in me, I guess." He leaned in to nuzzle the back of her ear again as she came more awake.

She finally blinked her eyes and stared down at his body. There was enough light coming between the curtains to create a soft glow in the room.

He didn't flinch when she trailed a hand over the scar on his leg like he did in the past with other women. Destiny knew about his scar. She'd seen it thousands of times. It was just part of him. A reminder of how dedicated Sean had been to him.

Her hand continued to dance up his body, stopping at the intricate Delta Force tattoo on his forearm. "You only have the one tattoo," she commented.

He shrugged. "I'm not much of a tattoo guy, but I couldn't deny at least the one when the rest of the team headed to the tattoo parlor." He wore it proudly, but he'd never felt addicted to ink.

She kissed a path up his arm reverently and then met his gaze. "It's gorgeous."

"Thank you." He scooted backward, pushing himself to sit against the headboard.

Destiny crawled up with him and snuggled into his side, unbothered by their nudity, which he loved.

It was time to share, and he prayed she wouldn't be mad about what he had to reveal. "Des..."

"Mmm."

"I need to show you something."

She lifted her gaze to his. "Okay." Her brow furrowed. "You look so serious."

He ran a hand up and down her back. "Yeah, it's important. I hope you won't be angry that I didn't show you sooner. I just didn't know when would be the right time, and we've been rushed every time we've seen each other."

She nodded slowly, her brows still drawn together.

Trent inhaled deeply and then leaned away from her

to reach over the side of the bed where he'd dropped his duffel bag. He tugged the worn letter still in the original envelope from the side pocket and then sat back up. He held it against his chest for a moment longer.

"What is it?" Destiny pushed up to sitting next to him.

"It's a letter from Sean. He wrote it three days before he died. I always felt like he had some sort of premonition or something. I didn't receive it until a week after his funeral."

She swallowed and then cleared her throat. "You want me to read it?"

"Yes. It's about you." He opened the envelope and extracted the single piece of notebook paper. Nothing fancy. Sean hadn't had stationary. He'd been in a war zone. Trent held it out to Destiny, his fingers shaking.

She met his gaze as she took it from him, and then she lowered her face, holding the paper with both hands.

Even though Trent knew every word from memory, he leaned over Destiny to read with her.

Trent,

I hope this letter gets to you. It's hard to say how crazy the mail might be from here. But I have some things weighing on my heart that I need to say in case I never get the chance in person.

First of all, I want you to know that you are the best brother a man could ever ask for. I know I haven't always been the easiest to live with. I know I'm uptight and too serious and introverted. I probably held you back on many occasions. But I want you to know how much it means to me that you've always been my best friend, dragging me out of my shell when needed, forcing me to leave my room and go out with you when you went to parties and met with friends. I realize most of our friends are really your friends, but you never once let me feel like they didn't enjoy hanging with me as much as you.

I'm laughing now as I remember the time you and me and Destiny snuck out of our houses late at night to catch lightning bugs. We were probably only eight years old. We threw rocks at Destiny's window because she fell asleep. We thought we were so sneaky, breaking all the rules, sneaking out after ten o'clock. I was hesitant, as usual, but you talked me into it, saying I needed to lighten up and live a little.

You were right. I know catching lightning bugs is a small thing, and I'm certain we didn't fool mom and dad for one second, but I think I laughed harder that night than any other time as we ran down the hill with our jars.

I know it's crazy and probably a little cheesy, but that was the night I think I first realized Destiny meant more to me than just a friend. I knew she was special even then. I loved her. I remember watching her run and jump and skip to catch the bugs, her wild curls flying in the night air. She had on pink pajamas and flip flops. Her giggle still makes me smile today. I miss her so much.

I've been selfish about her. I know that. I wanted her to like me more than you because she brings life to my ordinarily boring world. I know it was wrong of me to bulldoze you into agreeing that you were okay with me dating her.

I also know that you have always felt unnecessarily

beholden to me for going for help that day you fell and tore open your leg. There was no reason for you to think you owed me. You're my brother. My best friend in the world. The man I most admire. My flesh and blood. Of course, I ran to get help. I've never understood why you thought it was somehow heroic.

But I used that knowledge when I came to you and told you I wanted to ask her out. It wasn't fair. It was selfish and greedy. I guess I was desperate. Afraid one day soon someone else was going to snatch her up if one of us didn't. I wanted it to be me. So I claimed her.

I know you love her even more than I do. I've seen the way you look at her. I know I hurt you when I started dating her and changed the dynamic of our trio. I hate how you backed off from not just me but her, and I'm fully aware of why you had to do so. The pain in your eyes is always obvious.

The reason I'm saying all this is because I know I rushed things. I never should have asked her to marry me. It wasn't fair to any of us. Again, selfish. She loves you as much as you love her. The same pain I see on your face when you turn and walk another direction is mirrored on hers. She's not as happy and excited when she's alone with me. You bring that out in her.

I've made a mistake. I can also fix it. It's not too late. I love her dearly, but I'm not in love with her. Not like you are. I'm awkward with her. I enjoy spending time with her, but I don't have that spark that makes me think our marriage could work long-term.

She deserves more than I can give her. She deserves to be with you. She thrives on your exuberance. When you're around, she never stops talking and laughing. When she and I are alone, there are long periods of awkward silence.

Don't get me wrong. I know she loves me too, but not in the way a wife loves a husband. We don't quite fit that way.

Trent, I just want you to know that I'm sorry. I was only thinking of myself when I went down this path and couldn't seem to stop the freight train. I've been lying to myself and to Destiny and to you and mom and dad for months. The next time I'm on leave, I will break things off with her.

But Trent, just in case I don't make it home, I need you to promise me you will take care of her. I need you to be there for her. She will be hurting if I get killed. Even though she might not be in love with me, she will still hurt. Go to her. Be there for her. And eventually, make her yours. It's right.

Destiny has always been more yours than mine. Please make that happen. You two belong together. It was always meant to be that way.

Forgive me for my mistakes. I love both of you dearly. You are my life. All of my memories revolve around you two. Without you, my childhood would never have been as exciting.

If I'm home before you, I will fix this. If not, you can count on me to make this right as soon as I get there. But if something happens to me, I'm begging you to tell her. Show her this letter when the time is right.

Make her happy.

I love you.

Sean

Trent's throat was closed up as he read alongside Destiny. She hardly moved or breathed while she read, her gaze cast downward, her hair hanging down to obscure her face.

When she finished, she lowered the paper and lifted her head to face him. Silent tears were streaming down her face.

Trent felt every bit of her emotions. He too had cried reading this letter a hundred times. And his tears fell again now at the look on her face.

Finally, she set the letter aside, inhaled a choked sob, and leaned into him, burying her face in his shoulder and grasping his arm.

Trent wrapped his arms around her and held her tight as she cried hard. He rocked her back and forth, setting his chin on the top of her head. He didn't have the right to cry alongside her because he'd had twelve years to memorize those words. Words he should have shared with her a long time ago.

He'd been a coward for over a decade, thinking it would hurt her to see what Sean had written, believing Sean had been wrong and Destiny had truly loved him. The way she kept her distance from Trent and wouldn't meet his gaze or engage him in conversation spoke volumes. But Trent had misread her reaction.

The truth was so much more complicated. He felt bad for all the years they'd wasted in a misunderstanding.

Trent reached across Destiny's body to grab some tissue from the bedside table and hand it to her.

She finally leaned back, wiped her face, and

delicately blew her nose. When she looked at him, her face was splotchy and her eyes were red and swollen. She swallowed and whispered, "I get why you didn't share that before we got together, but why did you hold on to it for the last few weeks?"

He took a breath. "I don't know. At first, I wasn't ready. I didn't want our first few dates to be filled with pain and emotion. But a part of me also wanted to make sure that you cared about me as much as I hoped on its own merit without Sean's feelings being a factor." He stroked his palms up and down her arms. "I wanted you to fall for me without needing permission."

She hesitated and then slowly took a breath. "I can see that."

He pulled her into his embrace again. "You should have the letter. I've read it hundreds of times. I know it by heart. I'm certain Sean would want you to have it, and I know you'll want to read it again later."

She shook her head. "No. It's from your brother. His last words to you. But I'll take a picture so I can read it again."

He closed his eyes and smiled against her hair. Damn, she was perfect. After a few minutes, he spoke. "We should get dressed. I need to get to base."

She nodded and then kissed him quickly on the lips, lingering to stare into his eyes, before sliding off the bed and padding to the attached bathroom.

He heard the shower and plopped back down on the bed to stare at the ceiling. Relationships were hard and complicated. He was exhausted from sharing Sean's words and from worrying about what kind of future he could even have with Destiny. Woof had pounded into him that he deserved to be happy, but Trent still couldn't see any possible resolution that ended with him being safe and free to pursue love.

When Destiny returned, Trent rose and slid past her, cupping her cheek on the way by to make sure she was all right.

She smiled at him, not with the same happiness he liked to see on her face, but with the appropriate level of thoughtfulness and reverence for what she'd just found out.

When he returned to the bedroom, he found Destiny dressed and putting on her shoes. "Guess it won't do any good to ask when I might see you again."

"No. But I'll figure something out. Text me your schedule. I'll make something work." He shrugged into a pair of jeans and fastened them.

She finished tying her shoes and came toward him. Her hands flattened on his bare chest. "Maybe I was overreacting when I said we should sneak around and keep this relationship secret."

He held his breath a beat. He needed her to continue to feel that way for the time being. Finally, he lifted his hands to her arms and slid them up to her shoulders. "I think your idea has merit. It's easier than everyone finding out and grilling us about something we aren't ready to announce yet." He'd personally rather put their relationship on the main billboard coming into town—fuck everyone who judged either of them—but no way would he put her in danger like that.

She chewed on her bottom lip and then sighed.

"Yeah, more than anything, I'm not ready to face your parents and either disappoint them with my perceived unfaithfulness to your brother or excite them with *their* perceived second chance at securing me as a daughter."

Trent chuckled. "See? It's complicated. You made me understand. I get it. I'm behind you. We'll keep this on the down-low for a while longer. After all, we've been on exactly three dates now, and I took you to bed on the third date. I know my mother wouldn't approve." He chuckled to lighten the mood.

She smoothed her hands around to his pecs, her brows raised. "I hope you weren't planning on sharing such an intimate detail with your parents."

"Never." He grinned. "But it would be nearly impossible for us to go to my parents' house right now and them not see how obviously into you I am. I wouldn't be able to stop touching you and kissing you and holding you. They'd figure out we're much closer than three dates would presume."

She giggled. "We *are* much closer than three dates would presume. And I'm not sorry we had sex. Whew!" She fanned herself, making him smile. "But you're right. Your parents will be far more accepting if they don't know anything until we're certain." She bit her lip, holding his gaze.

He knew what she was silently asking. He could read her expression. Her eyes. *Aren't you certain*? And God yes, he was. Totally. But he wouldn't spill his heart right now this morning. He needed to fucking deal with the mission first. An apparent impossibility that made him feel like an ass for leading her on like this.

Destiny spoke again. "I promise not to question your whereabouts or doubt you. My insecurity is over."

"Good." He kissed her forehead, stepped back, and grabbed their bags. They exited the hotel in silence, and he walked her to her car. "I'll text you when I have a chance."

"I'll permit you to be cryptic."

He kissed her lips again. *God, I hate this so much.* He was lying by omission, and it sucked. He didn't give a single shit what anyone thought about him dating Destiny. And even though they were from a small town, it had been twelve years since people wasted time whispering about the biracial girl dating one of the town's hottest white boys. Times had changed, hadn't they? Trent couldn't imagine anyone doing a double-take seeing them together now.

On the other hand, he lived in different skin with different experiences. He enjoyed the privilege of being male and white. He couldn't step into her shoes and see the world through her eyes. However, if and when he ever got out from under his current mission and threat, he would take Destiny out in public in Killeen, and he would drive a fist into the first person to glance at them with disdain. That was not going to happen.

"Thanks for the best night of my life," she murmured against his neck.

"Des, you set the bar pretty low if that was the best night of your life. What comes in second? Your twenty-first birthday?" he teased.

"Uh-uh. The night you made me dinner. And then the night you came to Dallas." She kissed him one last time and slipped into the car before letting him respond.

He felt like he could walk on water as he watched her drive away. They hadn't said the exact words yet, but he was confident she knew how he felt, and he was equally certain she felt the same way.

CHAPTER 21

Trent paced the floor of the conference room on base, running a hand through his hair. "I'm not buying it."

"Neither are we," Merlin responded. "That's why we're meeting."

Turano crossed his arms and leaned against the wall, his eyebrows drawn together, his expression grim. He was just as frustrated as the rest of them.

Beyond exasperated, Trent stopped pacing and flattened his palms on the table so hard it shook. Not one of his team members flinched, however. He glanced at Turano. "So, let me get this straight, Commander. You're telling us that the ousted Kazarus government bombed the government buildings in Kazarus, killing the insurgents and taking back their country, and I'm supposed to believe that U.S. intelligence no longer sees Farid Demir as a threat?"

"I agree with Zip," Jangles said. "If Demir's brother and the rest of his family were killed in Kazarus, I'm inclined to believe he's angrier than ever. Is there any evidence he's left the country?"

Turano shook his head.

"Then we stay on alert," Merlin stated.

"More than ever," Woof agreed.

Duff scooted his chair back and stood. "Enough fucking chatting. Enough waiting for Demir to make his move. I say we hunt the fucker down and take him out."

Turano sighed and ran a hand down his face. "Not sure how long I can give you all the green light on this mission, so pick up the pace and stay quiet about it. Now get the fuck out of here."

All five of them rushed from the room. When they got to the parking lot, Merlin corralled them with hand motions. "Time to get proactive."

"Finally," Trent agreed. He was out of his mind stir-crazy. Besides the fact that he was tired of looking over his shoulder and hiding out while waiting, he'd been lying to Destiny for weeks now. She wouldn't tolerate his lame excuses much longer.

We switched sides, he reminded himself. It had been Destiny who wanted their relationship to remain secretive and hidden from the get-go. Trent regretted arguing with her that first night, insisting it wouldn't be necessary because now it was him using her excuse to continue the ruse. He'd freaked the fuck out with worry that he might've been followed to Lancelot yesterday even though two of his team had his back as he left Killeen. Trent was damn lucky they not only understood his predicament, but helped him hang on to his fledgling relationship in the midst of this insanity.

There was no way Trent could keep Destiny at arm's length much longer though. They'd discussed going to his parents just that morning, for Christ's sake. When Trent had protested lamely, Destiny had literally bitten her lip to hold back her thoughts, undoubtedly remembering how she'd doubted him already. He knew she didn't want to come off as needy and desperate.

Trent, on the other hand, would give anything to embrace her obvious change of heart. He couldn't wait for the day when he could bring her home to his parents, his hand on her waist, not holding back his affection. He knew in his heart his mother would be thrilled. It would also calm Destiny's nerves to out them to his parents at the very least. They could shout their feelings to the entire world after that. Trent had no hesitation.

One problem though, he reminded himself as he listened to Merlin's plan. He was lying to her. He prayed to God she would never find out about this mission and the danger he'd been dealing with for weeks now. The chance of him ever facing a threat this close to home again was nearly zero. It was unheard of. His identity had never been revealed in a mission before. And an enemy had never sent a hitman to the U.S. to seek revenge on any of them.

This morning's news changed everything. Onur Demir and everyone in his family had been killed. All Trent needed to do was capture Farid and there wouldn't be anyone left to care about hunting down Trent.

If Farid disappeared into the wind, however, backing

off to lick his wounds, or even leaving the country to bury his family, Trent would never feel safe. He would always be looking over his shoulder, waiting for Farid to come back for revenge.

That wasn't an option. They had to find him.

Trent had longed for a chance with Destiny half his life. He didn't want it screwed up by bad timing. He preferred she maintain some romanticized vision of him fighting bad guys overseas or protecting good guys. He hated for her to know his shit had blown back to follow him home. He didn't want any civilian to know about this. Not his parents *or* Destiny. He never wanted them to panic in the future, or to spend their lives worried that someone might kill him or them right in their own hometown. It would change everything if they carried that weight around with them.

Honestly, Trent felt guilty for even meeting up with Destiny on the sly. He was endangering her a little more every time. He couldn't keep this up. He hadn't seen his parents for a few weeks either, and before that only on base where they could come and go without anyone realizing who they were seeing.

Granted, Farid Demir might have known more about Trent than he gave the man credit for. A chill raced down Trent's spine when he considered the possibility that Demir had been tailing Trent for weeks, watching, waiting for someone to get sloppy. He knew they would. And he was right.

Commander Turano agreed enough about the existence of the threat to permit his team to continue pursuing Demir, but for how long? Another week?

Two? Eventually, if they had no leads, they would be pulled off and sent on another mission.

And where would that leave Destiny? Trent would fear for her safety indefinitely. He could hold her off from going public for a few more weeks at the most, and then she was going to accuse him of being ashamed of her. He could already see the worry forming in her eyes every time he saw her.

Trent shook his thoughts from his head to focus on what Merlin was saying. "Let's split up, hit every hotel in the area. We know what rental car he's driving. We have the tag number, make, and model. He can't be sleeping in his car for weeks. I'll get the clearance so we can check the guest list at the hotels, and then we'll move to restaurants. It could be tedious work, but I for one am done sitting around."

"Agreed." Duff nodded.

"Great. Duff, you're with me. Jangles, see what you can find out on that rental. Maybe he's turned it back in or exchanged it. Woof, you're with Zip." Merlin paused, his gaze on Trent. "Failing this, you ready to up the stakes?"

"Yep."

Merlin nodded. "Let's get to it then."

Everyone moved.

Trent's body felt heavy as he climbed into the passenger side of Woof's SUV. They'd worked together on many assignments so they no longer paused to decide who would drive and who would navigate. They'd grown to know how they best complemented each other.

After Woof pulled out of the parking lot, he glanced at Trent. "This is wearing on you."

"It is." Trent sighed.

"You sure you're in favor of plan B?"

"Yes." Trent glanced at Woof. They'd all known that eventually, their best bet would be for Trent to stop hiding and put himself out there. It was never their first choice, but the clock was ticking before the entire mission would be yanked out from under them and abandoned. As much as Trent didn't relish the idea of walking around town like a giant target with a bullseye on his chest, he hated dragging this out indefinitely even more.

"You still haven't told Destiny about this threat, have you?"

"Nope. Not going to."

"You think that's wise? No one would blame you if you warned her. You might even be able to convince her to stay in Dallas for a while."

Trent shook his head. He'd gone over this a thousand times in his mind. "Not gonna happen. If she finds out, she'll never feel safe. I don't want that for her. We just got together after twelve years of misunderstanding. I don't want my first mission after clearing the air to be one that puts her in danger."

"But it *is*. Maybe she's strong enough to handle it."

"Would you tell Nori if it were her life in danger?" Woof's relationship with Nori was new, too. He would understand. Lucky for him, Nori was currently working overseas.

Woof winced. "I get it. I do. But it's hard to know the

answer to that hypothetical. Maybe she would be okay with it."

"Well, I can't take that risk." Trent had gone over this dozens of times in his mind. It was true that Destiny was a strong woman, stronger than he'd ever known or given her credit for. There was no doubt in his mind she could handle almost anything. He didn't even believe she would walk away from him if she knew someone was trying to kill him. She wasn't that kind of woman. The problem was that once he told her, she would forever worry. Look over her shoulder. Fear would follow her everywhere.

No. I won't do that to her. He wanted to catch this asshole, end his existence, and return to Destiny with her innocence intact.

CHAPTER 22

After pouring through the registered guests at five local hotels, Trent was frustrated and exhausted. No one at any hotel currently had a guest who fit Farid Demir's description. No one recognized his photo. Although a few hotels had guests of Middle Eastern descent, none of them remembered a guest with a Kazarian accent.

They were going to have to expand their search to include neighboring towns next. When they checked in with Commander Turano, he confirmed that Demir still had not left the country, not by conventional means at least. The man would surely have made his way to Killeen from Dallas. It wouldn't take any effort for a man like him to figure out that Trent lived there. His address had probably been easy to track down, even though he'd made every effort to keep his location private when he moved in. Which meant Trent believed there was a good chance Farid was watching him. Waiting. Plotting.

But, at least he might be out of Dallas, where Destiny lived.

Trent's phone pinged, indicating an incoming text as he climbed back into Woof's SUV. He lifted the cell, a rush of emotions bombarding him when he saw the message was from Destiny. Every time she contacted him, he was both elated and nervous.

Hey. Just wanted you to know I'm thinking about you. I'm still off until tomorrow if you want to meet somewhere again tonight. I hope I don't sound desperate. I just hated driving away this morning. I totally understand if you have to work.

Trent closed his eyes, gritting his teeth. He wanted to tell her he'd be there in two hours. He wanted to tell her he would stay a week. He wanted to stop sneaking around, meeting up with her like she was some kind of booty call, because she most definitely was not.

That sounds so much better than working all night, but I'm going to have to take a raincheck. I'm on a lead.

She responded immediately.

Okay. That sounds like a good thing. Right? I mean, usually you seem to be waiting, like this thing has a lot of dead ends. Maybe it's wrapping up.

He pursed his lips as he sent back a reply.

I sure hope so. I'm tired of this mission. I'll text or call as soon as I can. Be safe.

You too.

Her response was so short. He could almost see her sighing in frustration. He couldn't blame her. He wouldn't date him. Not in a million years. Not even if he'd known himself for most of his life. That didn't change the fact that despite being proud that he kept Americans safe, his job sucked right now. Big time.

"You good?" Woof asked.

"Yeah." Trent knew he didn't sound good, nor did he feel good, but he had to put Destiny out of his mind and focus on this damn mission. His life wasn't his own until he found Farid Demir and stopped him.

Woof's phone rang through the vehicle's speakers and he answered it. "Talk to me."

"Woof, it's Duff, you with Zip?"

"I'm here," Trent responded.

"We hit every hotel on our list. Nothing."

"Us too," Woof told him.

"Let's head to Jangles' place and make a plan," Duff suggested.

"Be there in twenty," Woof responded. He glanced at Trent as he ended the call. "You sure about this?"

"Very." He was out of options. He wanted this asshole picked up, dead or alive. All he could do now was pray he didn't end up in a body bag himself.

Trent spent the entire twenty minutes staring out the window and pondering how they were going to proceed. By the time they arrived at Jangles', everyone else was there. They didn't waste time or words. Each grabbed a bottle of water and perched around Jangles' living room. His cat, Buster, was sitting on Woof's lap, making the big man look soft as he petted the little rescue. He'd been the one to find her and bring her to Jangles, and it seemed the furball never forgot it.

Trent spoke first. "Don't even question me. I'm all-in. I want this done." He needed to put Destiny out of his mind and focus. Exposing himself intentionally was a huge risk, but the clock was ticking. If Farid was still in town, he would probably go dark soon. That was unacceptable.

Yes, there were enormous risks to flushing Demir out. Yes, there was a chance Trent would be killed. Yes, he was a fucking asshole for sleeping with Destiny and letting her fall in love with him. If he died, she would be devastated. It was ironic that Sean described himself as selfish. Apparently, both brothers were selfish when it came to Destiny. He knew it would destroy her to lose him, too. So, he couldn't let it happen.

Merlin dropped a map on the coffee table, and they all leaned over it. He set his pointer at the location they'd already discussed days ago, preparing for this eventuality.

"It's a Sunday. There won't be many people in the vicinity of this strip mall. Since it's in a business district, nothing is open on Sundays."

Duff reached out to tap a specific corner. "There's a deli right here. You'll drive there, park, and then wander toward the entrance. If you glance around and check your watch a few times, it will easily look like you were meeting someone there and didn't realize it's not open."

Trent nodded. "Who's going to inform Roe?"

"Already did," Jangles stated. "While we were waiting for you. He hated it, but he gave us the green light. I don't think he believes Farid is still in the area, so he's hoping we'll let this go after we prove him correct."

Trent took a deep breath, expanding his chest. He disagreed with the commander on this one. He'd been walking around with goose bumps for weeks. Usually, his instincts were dead-on. Trent had felt like Farid was one step behind him every day. The only thing holding him back was that he hadn't been given an opportunity. Today, he would have his chance.

Woof handed Trent a vest and a reinforced ball cap. "Don't you dare go all heroic. Put these on. I don't care how fucking hot you are or how heavy they get. Do it." He lifted a brow.

Trent glared at him as he snagged the vest and cap. "I don't have a death wish. Trust me. Not leaving the apartment without protection."

"Good." Merlin glanced around. "Everyone ready?"

They all nodded and stood.

"Let's do this," Merlin added.

CHAPTER 23

Trent wished Woof hadn't reminded him how fucking hot and heavy the damn vest was going to be. The reinforced ball cap was no better. Sweat dripped down the back of Trent's neck. He might've stood a better chance ignoring the two extra articles of clothing without the reminder. As it was, he was stuck standing outside the deli, his hand lifted against the glare of the sun, scanning the area. He prayed he appeared to be looking for a friend. If Farid caught wind or got spooked, he would pass right on by.

After the meeting at Jangles' house, Trent had returned to his place, pulling up alongside Woof and then hiding in his friend's shadow to get inside. That part wasn't difficult. Although there were plenty of places where Farid could be lurking day after day, keeping tabs on Trent coming and going, it would be nearly impossible to get a shot in between the parking spot and the building. Too many obstacles in the way.

The bushes were high, and there were mailboxes and trash cans and partial walls near the entrance.

Trent had never really expected to get picked off at his own apartment. The concern had been for every time he left and was followed. Never once had any of the five of them seen anything suspicious, though. If this plan today failed, Trent feared Farid would never be taken out.

As planned, Trent had left his apartment fifteen minutes later, sauntering to his car in the wide open, his aim to lure Farid into following him.

Now, Trent was standing in the wide-open, pacing in front of a restaurant that wasn't open. He knew exactly where his team members were positioned, scanning the area and watching him like a hawk. *But where the fuck is Farid*?

"Fuck," Trent muttered, knowing everyone would hear him through the comm in his ear. "Where are you, asshole?" He scanned the area again. It had been five minutes since he arrived. Sweat was running down his back now. The button-up shirt he wore to conceal the vest was sticking to his biceps in the afternoon sun. He was at a disadvantage that he hated by the angle of the sun at this hour. It shouldn't matter though, since he wasn't expected to be the one to take out Farid. His team would do that as soon as they spotted Farid approaching.

Five more long minutes passed before Merlin spoke. "Got him. He's coming from the west, driving slowly. Car and plates match the description. Where has this fucker been hiding?" he asked rhetorically.

"I see him," Woof added. "Don't change your location, but move around a bit, and tug that hat down. I'm not losing a fucking team member today, Zip."

Trent adjusted his cap, not at all interested in getting shot, either. He started pacing to the left and then the right, listening for the engine. "Someone gonna take him out? Now would be good," he suggested into the com.

"Fuck," Merlin responded. "I don't have a shot. Jangles?"

"Negative. Woof?"

Trent could hear Woof breathing heavily as he spoke. "I need ten seconds to get into a better position. I think I can take him."

"We don't have ten fucking seconds," Duff shouted into everyone's earpiece. "We need to move now. He's about to round the corner."

Trent could see the car now as he slowly turned onto the street. About a half a dozen other cars were driving by in both directions, but none of them would stop at this closed strip mall.

"I'm coming up behind him," Woof informed them. "Praying he doesn't see me at his rear."

"Can anyone confirm if he's alone?" Trent asked.

"Affirmative," Merlin responded. "I don't have sight on a weapon yet. Maybe he's testing you. Look to the right so he doesn't think you're onto him."

The moment Trent followed that last instruction, there was a loud screech of tires. He knew instinctively even before jerking his gaze toward Farid that the man had slammed on the gas and swerved onto the sidewalk at full speed, aiming straight for Trent.

For a moment, Trent was certain Farid was going to ram into him and pin him against the front of the deli. But then the rear of the car spun sideways out of control. Farid yanked the door open and jumped from the car.

Trent heard the first shot before he saw the gun. He pulled his weapon out to angle it toward where Farid was crouched down behind the driver's side door.

"Fuck," Woof yelled. "Duck. I need five seconds to come up behind him."

Trent didn't obey that last directive. Instead, he lifted his gun, angled it at the car, and fired off two rounds. He had to be careful. They couldn't afford to have a civilian get caught in the crossfire. Trent was at a severe disadvantage since he was open bait.

Three more shots rang out in quick succession. Trent wasn't sure who fired them. Everyone on his team was shouting in his ear, but he couldn't make out anything specific.

The next shot shocked Trent when it hit him square in the chest from a weapon that packed a larger than average punch. As he staggered backward, another shot hit him in the leg. *That* fucking hurt. He grabbed his thigh as he went down onto his knees, took aim, and fired several rounds at Farid with as much precision as he could.

He knew he only had a few rounds left when Farid managed to graze his head. Trent's ears started ringing and he lost his equilibrium. He swayed backward, knowing his best bet now was to flatten to the ground.

That was his last coherent thought.

CHAPTER 24

Destiny had been home for several hours when Libby shouted at her from downstairs. She'd been folding laundry and cleaning her room, energized from the best night of her life, smiling, happy, relaxed.

Libby screamed a moment later, and Destiny dropped the shirt she was putting on a hanger and ran for the stairs. She found Libby standing in the middle of the living room in front of the television. "Destiny," she yelled, not realizing Destiny was already behind her.

"What?" Destiny stepped next to her roommate and shifted her gaze to whatever had captured Libby's attention on the screen. She had no idea what she was looking at, but it was obviously a crime scene. There were dozens of police officers and flashing lights and ambulances and fire trucks. People were standing behind crime scene tape.

The next thing that caught Destiny's eye was the blue square in the right-hand corner of the screen, indicating this active crime was in Killeen, Texas. She sucked in a breath and scanned the screen while the reporter revealed several injuries and one fatality.

Destiny grabbed Libby's arm when she saw Jangles in the corner. She sucked in a breath and froze when she noticed Merlin was with him.

Destiny's knees wobbled, and she lowered herself to the sofa.

Libby helped her with a grip on her arm. "What's the matter?" she murmured.

"Trent is there."

"How do you know?"

"I saw two of his teammates."

Libby rubbed her arm. "Okay. Take a breath. I'm sure he's fine."

Destiny couldn't tear her gaze from the television. She couldn't catch her breath, either. A moment later, her cell phone buzzed in her back pocket, and she struggled with shaking fingers to extract it, praying it was a coincidence she would get a call right now.

The screen read *Trent,* and she blew out a breath in relief as she answered the call. "Trent?"

"Destiny?"

The voice did not belong to Trent.

"Yes?" Her response was shaking. "Who is this? Where's Trent?"

"This is Woof. He's been injured. I grabbed his phone as they loaded him in the ambulance. I'll text you the information for the hospital." The call ended so fast that Destiny wasn't sure it had even happened. She was still staring at the cell when a text came through, making her jump.

There was no mistaking the incoming text though.

"Come on," Libby said, hauling Destiny to her feet. "I'll drive."

Destiny couldn't remember much about getting to the car or the drive. Libby kept a polite line of conversation, glancing at Destiny every few seconds, but Destiny could do nothing but stare out the window and pray to God Woof hadn't lied to her. There was one casualty. *Please let it not be Trent.*

The two hours it took to get to the Fort Hood Medical Center were interminable. Libby pulled right up to the emergency entrance. "I'll park and meet you inside."

Destiny yanked the door open and rushed toward the sliding double doors. She glanced around. The room was packed with people. She searched for a familiar face. Before she could find someone who might have answers, she heard Trent's name coming from a guy near her and froze.

He was with another man and the two of them left through a side door.

Destiny followed them, knowing they'd have information she might have trouble getting otherwise.

Sure enough, a minute later, the two men entered another waiting room. Destiny continued walking right past the smaller room, glancing only long enough to see it was filled with Trent's teammates and who she assumed were other military personnel. She stopped moving when she was past the door, heart pounding.

It was wrong to eavesdrop, but she didn't think there was any other way she might get more information about Trent. These guys were Delta. They wouldn't be able to tell her much of anything.

She wanted to round the corner, press her way into their group, and demand information, but she hesitated, deciding she might become more informed if she listened instead.

"What happened?" someone asked.

"Things went south, obviously." She recognized the voice as Merlin's. He kept his voice low, but Destiny was close enough to hear him. "Trent had hoped to flush out the hitman and take him out before he had a chance to strike, Commander. But this fucker was prepared. He had a lot of ammunition and we couldn't get a good shot, and he was able to shoot off several rounds at Trent before we stopped him."

Destiny's head spun. *What the hell? A hitman?*

The commander cursed under his breath. "I can't believe this asshole eluded us for weeks and then got the upper hand."

Destiny sucked in a breath. *Weeks?* The mission Trent had been so secretive about had included a man hunting him down for weeks? She didn't realize she'd closed her eyes and was gritting her teeth until someone's hand landed on her shoulder. "Destiny?"

She tipped her head back to meet Merlin's gaze. Another man was standing next to him.

Merlin was frowning. "I didn't see you out here in the hallway. You okay?"

No. She wasn't okay. She was furious. She also knew she wasn't going to get more details out of anyone. It would be classified. Everything was fucking classified.

But this... Jesus. Her voice squeaked. "Trent knew this? He knew someone wanted to kill him, and he didn't tell me?"

The other man spoke. "Destiny, I'm Woof. I'll fill you in."

She shot him a glare. She'd heard about Woof, knew he was on Trent's team, but right now she wasn't in the mood to meet his other teammates. She wanted answers.

Woof cringed. "You overheard us talking," he realized out loud.

Ya think?

Woof sighed. "Trent didn't want you to worry."

"He didn't want me to *worry*?" Her voice rose. She didn't give a fuck. "Someone's been trying to kill him and he didn't *tell* me?" Dozens of thoughts raced through her mind, bombarding her.

How he kept meeting her in hiding.

How he'd thought she was overreacting when she suggested they keep their relationship secret but then changed his mind and went along with her.

How he'd held back his feelings when they were together, when she'd been certain he loved her as much as she loved him.

It all fell into place. He'd been trying to protect her. But he'd gone too far. He'd expected her to trust him while he hadn't extended that courtesy to her. How could he keep this from her? The secrecy of his job she could understand. But not this kind of mission. Not one where he'd been lying in wait because someone wanted him dead.

"He should have told me," she muttered to herself.

"I agree. But he didn't. He'd hoped you would never find out."

"The shooter?"

"Dead."

"Anyone else?"

"Several cars driving by ended up in two accidents, but no one was seriously injured. We strategically picked a spot where no civilians would be nearby today."

"What are his injuries?" She needed information, and then she needed to get out of here before she lost it and started screaming or crying. She just needed to know he would be okay.

"He was wearing a vest and a reinforced cap. He'll have a nasty bruise and a few broken ribs from a shot to the chest. Another bullet grazed his head, so he suffered a concussion and a ruptured eardrum. Both of those will heal." Woof's voice lowered. "The third bullet hit his femur. That's what they're repairing in surgery now."

"Prognosis?" She had no idea why she was able to so coherently ask all these questions. Some part of her was close to falling apart. But she managed to continue to hold it together for a few more minutes.

"They say he should be fine. The main artery wasn't severed." Woof was frowning at her. "You okay?"

"Peachy." She glanced away from him. "I have to go." She took a step back.

"Go?" Woof reached for her.

Destiny jumped back several feet. "You seem to think he'll live. That's all I needed to know. Tell him…

Tell him to have a nice life." She spun around and rushed back through the hospital, spotting Libby near the entrance. She met her friend's gaze as she passed, knowing Libby would follow her out the door.

"Destiny?" Libby rushed to catch up, grabbing Destiny's arm in the parking lot. "What's going on?"

"He's gonna live."

"So, where are we going?"

"Home."

"Why would we do that?"

"Because he lied to me. He didn't trust me to handle this fucking mission he'd been involved in. I can tolerate a lot of things, but not him coddling me as if I'm not made of the stuff it takes to be with a Delta." Destiny spun and continued stomping across the parking lot. She had no idea where the car was. She just wanted to get as far away from the hospital as she could.

A woman shouted Destiny's name from behind, making her turn around. Destiny's heart nearly screeched to a halt when she saw Trent's mom, Nancy, rushing toward her. "Destiny?" she repeated when she got closer.

"Nancy..." Destiny hadn't used a more formal 'Mrs. Dawkins' to address Trent's mom from the moment she'd moved next door and the woman insisted she call her Nancy.

Nancy was out of breath when she reached Destiny and Libby. Her eyebrows were drawn together in confusion. "What are you doing here? How did you know about...? I mean, of course you're here, but..."

Every ounce of strength Destiny had been holding

on to for the past fifteen minutes dissolved in an instant and she lurched forward and wrapped her arms around Nancy. "God, I'm so sorry. This must be so hard for you." She hugged the woman tight.

Nancy nodded. Tears were in her eyes as she pulled back and met Destiny's gaze. "It is, but they say the surgery is going well. He should be fine." She looked so confused. "Were you on his call list or something? I didn't realize you two were even in contact in the last several years."

Destiny nodded, not sure what she wanted to say to Nancy. Part of her wanted to spill the entire saga and cry endlessly in the woman's arms. A woman who'd been a second mother to her for most of her formative years. She couldn't do it, though. She couldn't tell Nancy anything. It would give the woman hope where none existed now. Trent hadn't trusted Destiny. That was inexcusable. She simply swallowed. "We were in contact sometimes. I guess he had my number in his phone."

Nancy nodded slowly. "Did you drive here from Dallas?" She glanced at Libby.

Libby cleared her throat. "I drove her, ma'am. I'm her roommate."

Destiny was grateful Libby didn't elaborate.

"Are you leaving already?" Nancy asked.

"Yeah… I had to know that he was okay. I was worried. It was silly for me to drive here. I should have just called you." She forced herself to sound nonchalant. "I need to get back to Dallas. I have to work." She bit the inside of her lip, hoping the pain would distract her long enough to hold it together.

Nancy stared at her a moment and then smiled wanly. "Okay, well, I have your number. I'll text you updates."

"That would be nice." Destiny forced a smile.

"You're sure you don't want to stay awhile? We could have a coffee while we wait. It would be a nice distraction. We could catch up a bit. I haven't seen you in a while. I've missed you."

Destiny hugged her again. "I've missed you too." That was more true than Nancy would ever know. Destiny had missed Trent's mom almost as much as she'd missed the guys themselves after she cut herself off and left town. She still saw Nancy and William from time to time, briefly, but she always made excuses and retreated quickly, unable to stand the pain of the immense loss of the entire Dawkins family. She leaned back, holding Nancy's arms. "I can't stay, but I'll be in touch soon," she lied. Her heart was breaking, shattering as she spoke. She needed to get back to the car where she could fall apart without making a scene.

Nancy nodded. "Okay, hon. I'll tell Trent you were here. I'm sure he'll be glad to know you came by."

I'm sure he'll throw several things across the hospital room and scream loud enough to shake the building. But that wasn't Destiny's problem. Trent had made his bed. Now he could lie in it. Alone.

CHAPTER 25

Everything hurt.

Trent blinked his eyes several times until he could avoid squinting in the bright lights. The scent of disinfectant and the sound of beeping told him exactly where he was. His last memories flooded back quickly, too.

He knew he'd been hit by at least one bullet, but obviously, he'd lived.

"Nancy, he's awake." The muffled voice belonged to Trent's father, William, and his face loomed over Trent moments later.

"Thank God," his mother responded as she clasped his hand on the other side of the bed. He could hear her more clearly.

He shifted his gaze to face her, wincing when pain stabbed his temple, forcing him to close his eyes again.

"Don't try to speak yet, Trent," she soothed, gripping his hand. "Take your time. You're in the hospital. You're going to be okay."

He swallowed, but his mouth was too dry.

"Here," his father said, "Ice chips."

Trent squinted at the concerned expression on his father's face as he accepted the slivers of ice. They felt good on his tongue and soothed his throat, too. He opened his mouth to accept more. Even his jaw hurt.

"Ah, you're awake." The new voice came from the foot of the bed, and Trent attempted to glance that way, but couldn't move his head without causing excruciating pain. "I'm Dr. Sullivan. I operated on your leg."

Trent's father stepped out of the way, and Dr. Sullivan leaned into Trent's line of sight. He was tall, broad, and bald. His skin was dark, and his eyes were genuine. He offered Trent a smile before flashing an unwelcome light in one eye and then the other. "I'll give you a rundown. The worst shot was to your femur. I removed the fragments and stabilized the bone. You'll have a nice scar on the top of your leg to match the one you already have. You'll need physical therapy for a few months for it to fully heal."

"My head is killing me," Trent finally managed to whisper.

The doctor nodded. "Bullet grazed the side of your head. The reinforced cap saved you from a nasty scar. No skin was broken, but your eardrum ruptured. That should heal in about a month. You suffered a concussion, but I suspect that happened when you lost consciousness and fell. Nasty bruise on your chest is going to be very sore for a few weeks also. You took a direct hit to the chest. Thank God you were wearing the vest. You wouldn't be here otherwise."

"The shooter?"

"Dead," the doctor confirmed.

Trent let his eyes slide closed and breathed out slowly. *Thank God.*

"I'll let your parents visit a few more minutes, and your team members are in the hallway waiting to make sure you're okay. They won't leave until you prove I'm not lying." He chuckled.

Destiny... Did anyone call Des?

The doctor left, and Trent's mother smoothed a hand over his head. "You scared us to death."

"Sorry. Wasn't my plan," he managed to murmur.

She gave him a forced smile. "Well, your humor is still intact."

It hurt too much to return the smile or even nod.

"We should let him rest," his father said. "I'll tell your team they can pop in."

"You'll feel much better after a solid night's sleep," his mother added, leaning over him to kiss his forehead. "Oh, I almost forgot, Destiny was here. She couldn't stay, but she wanted to make sure you were okay. I didn't realize you two were in communication lately. Someone must have called her."

Trent's entire body stiffened. *She was here. She left...*

His mother gave his hand one last squeeze and moved so that his team could crowd around him. Every one of them touched some part of his body, expressing their relief that he was going to be fine and joking that he'd be running circles around them and cracking jokes before they could get out of bed tomorrow.

He appreciated their banter, but his mind was on Destiny. He searched for Woof among the faces, his head splitting with pain to do so. When he met his gaze, he asked about a dozen questions with his eyes.

The rest of the guys gave a final pat, nod, or squeeze and disappeared, leaving Woof the only one in the room. He leaned over Trent, not meeting his gaze until he took a deep breath. "She was pissed," he finally admitted.

Trent nodded slightly, his chest hurting from far more than the impact of the bullet.

"Once she got over the initial fear, I tried to explain your reasoning, but she was too hurt and angry to listen to me."

"You spoke to her here?" Trent murmured.

"Yes. She saw the entire thing on the news and her roommate drove her here. She was lost and scared out of her mind. But after she found out you would survive, she just… Man, I'm so sorry."

Trent swallowed, his teeth gritting. He'd made this bed. Now he had to lie in it.

CHAPTER 26

Two weeks later…

Trent eased himself onto the sofa in his parents' living room as his mom scurried around him to arrange pillows so he could prop up his leg. The bulky brace was cumbersome and annoying, but the doctor insisted it was mandatory for at least eight weeks.

The dark bruising on Trent's chest was fading to yellow finally, and his hearing was slowly starting to return to normal. For the first several days, everything sounded underwater. The ENT said the rupture was healing; it just needed time.

His body was mending. His heart was in tatters.

Trent's mother bustled around him, adding pillows and ensuring he could reach drinks and snacks on the TV tray she set up next to him. "There." She clapped her hands together, looking pleased for about a moment, and then she sat on the coffee table next to him and furrowed her brow. "Talk to me."

He shot her a confused look, one eyebrow raised. "About what?"

"I know you hit your head, but that's healing. I'm sure your chest is sore and your thigh is throbbing. There's a ringing in your ear that's probably driving you slowly mad also. But you've never once in your life been as defeated as you've been for the last two weeks."

He pursed his lips.

She continued. "I'm sure it's also frustrating that you've had to take time off from your team to heal. That's understandable. I know what Delta Force means to you. However, my upbeat, joking, happy, outgoing son has vanished without a trace, and I want to know why."

Damn, she's perceptive. He stared at her, wondering if she'd also been this perceptive a dozen years ago when Destiny started dating and got engaged to the wrong brother. "Mom, I'm fine."

"Uh-huh. That's how you want to play this? Because from my vantage point, you're kinda trapped here with me doting on you hand and foot for a few weeks. So, I can either badger you daily, or you can just spill the beans and let me help you fix whatever has you so disgruntled."

He rolled his eyes and leaned his head back.

"Let me take a stab in the dark here. Does this have anything to do with a certain Destiny Fisher?"

Trent couldn't stop his body from flinching at the

mention of Destiny's name coming from his mother's lips, and how damn perceptive she'd proven to be.

"Ah-ha. Now we're getting somewhere. I wondered. She seemed very out of sorts when I saw her the day of your accident. It's been bugging me ever since. Now that we've eliminated the mystery, it's your turn to talk."

He lifted one hand and rubbed his eyes with his thumb and middle finger. "Mom, I'd rather not."

She didn't respond for several long moments, and then she blew out an audible breath and slouched forward a bit. "You know, I always wondered what happened between you two."

"Mom..." he warned.

"You don't have to talk. Just listen." His mom settled in. "You had an eye for her from a very young age. So did your brother. Even though you three were close friends starting in kindergarten, it didn't take long to notice there was a silent rivalry for her time and her attention. It worried me. I was afraid you two would eventually fight over her and it would destroy your close relationship as brothers and best friends."

Trent stared at the ceiling. It was amazing how insightful she'd been. He should have known.

"I was never quite sure if Destiny felt the same way toward either of you. She gave you equal attention. I know it was partly because she was an old soul who knew in her heart at a young age that she should not pick favorites. And besides, it didn't matter. You two were so different that you each had your own separate relationship with her. Sean could talk to her about serious book stuff, and you could make her laugh and discuss more abstract concepts."

Trent squeezed his eyes closed, wishing she would stop while wanting to hear her assessment at the same time.

"When Destiny was with Sean, she was a leader. When she was with you, she was a follower. It made sense. It was also intriguing. A social scientist would have had a field day watching the dynamic you all had. Neither of you ever got jealous or spiteful. And then Sean asked her out."

Trent threw his forearm over his eyes now, concerned he might actually start crying.

"Worried me to death. I watched you retreat, and I prayed to God you did so to be polite, all the while worrying you were hurting inside. I should have talked to you. It was wrong of me to get so damn excited over their relationship and later engagement while you were silently glowering in the corner."

"I was not glowering. Be real," he finally added, not moving his arm or lifting his face.

She chuckled. "You so totally were."

Okay, maybe I was.

"I watched Destiny like a hawk, too, trying to make sure she wasn't making a mistake, but I couldn't be sure. All I could do was hope if she consented to marry Sean, it was for the right reasons. Inside, I was so happy. I love that girl with all my heart. I love her as if she were my own child. She spent more time here than in her own home when her grandmother had to work when you were young, coming over after school, doing homework at our table, eating dinner with us at times. I love her, and it clouded my vision."

"Mom..." The one word came out choked. He was going to become a ball of emotions in a moment.

She ignored his protest. "I decided not to worry about the engagement. After all, no dates were set, and there was plenty of time for the two of them to be certain about their feelings." Her voice dipped. "And then Sean was killed, and my life broke into little pieces, and I was so depressed over the death of my sweet, gentle boy that I couldn't focus on anyone else. You were home for the funeral, but then you had to go back. Destiny was here too, but it was too painful for her, and she moved to Dallas. I don't see her nearly as often as I'd like to. It hurts. I lost two kids that day."

A tear slid from the corner of Trent's eye, and he rubbed it against his forearm.

"You and Destiny never mended whatever was broken. That made me sad too, but I stayed out of it. And then when I saw her at the hospital, I knew something was up. She was so distressed. Furious, in fact. Her demeanor stood out to me in a way that I couldn't stop thinking about. I would have expected her to be worried or sad or crying or something. Instead, she was angry. Why, Trent? Please tell me what I've missed."

It took him a moment to find his voice, and even then, it was broken and soft. "Go in my room and open the side pocket of my duffel. There's a letter in there from Sean. You should read it. But do it alone. Take your time."

"Trent?"

"Please, Mom."

"Okay, honey." She stood and leaned over him, forcing him to meet her gaze. "I love you with all my heart, you know."

"I know, Mom."

After a moment, she rose and padded from the room.

Trent's heart beat wildly in his chest while she was gone. And she was gone a damn long time. Half an hour or more.

When she finally returned, he was sitting up straighter. He was certain his face was red from silently crying, but hers was splotchy and swollen. She had the saddest eyes he'd ever seen. "Oh, honey..."

Trent swallowed renewed emotion and nodded. "Yeah."

His mother leaned over him and hugged him hard, rocking gently for a long time. When she pulled back, she met his gaze. "Has Destiny read that?"

"Yes. Recently."

She furrowed her brow.

There was no way he could continue putting his mother off. "We ran into each other at the Ugly Mug about two months ago. She'd been avoiding me for all these years. A giant misunderstanding stood in the way of us ever speaking to each other. She finally had the guts to face me head-on and spill a decade of pent-up frustration."

His mother smiled. "That sounds like Destiny."

He tried to return the smile, knowing it was a lame

attempt. "Not going to lie, she was a bit drunk." That was an understatement. "Tequila did the talking."

His mother chuckled. "Tequila will do that. Sometimes it can be a good thing."

"Seemed like it to me at the time. Turns out while I've spent all these years thinking she couldn't face me because I reminded her of Sean, a man she'd been very much in love with, she'd spent all this time embarrassed to admit that she'd known she'd made a mistake because she'd been in love with me."

His mother gasped. Her hand came to her mouth, and she pressed her fingers against her lips.

"Yeah, that was my reaction. That and heart-stopping elation that the woman I'd been pining over for half my life was doing the same for me."

His mother's eyes widened, and she lowered her hand. "So, did you start seeing her?"

"Yes. Sort of. But we had a mountain of problems. For one, she's concerned about what people will think. She doesn't want the town to think ill of her for switching brothers. She has some deep-rooted, built-in fears about the fact that she's biracial. She's fought hard in a mostly white world to be seen as good enough."

His mother frowned. "That makes me so sad."

"Yeah, and I felt like an idiot for not realizing it. To me, she's just Destiny, the sweet, adorable girl from next door with the amazing, gorgeous skin and curly hair and beautiful, dark eyes."

The smile that spread on his mother's face made Trent close his eyes a moment.

"Anyway, she didn't want to jump the gun and

out our burgeoning relationship to the town, worrying about how they would gossip about us if we didn't manage to end up together. Also," Trent paused to capture his mother's gaze. "She was worried about you and Dad, afraid you would either think ill of her for defiling her relationship with Sean—"

She flinched. "I would never do that."

"Yeah, well, she also worried you would be so elated to have her back in the fold that you would pick out china before we even had a chance to go on a single real date."

His mother chuckled. "Now *that* I would do. But please tell me you tried to talk her down."

"Of course, I did, and then I found out about this threat against my life."

"Oh."

"And I made a pile of mistakes. I should have told her. I realize that now. I've had two weeks to think about my stupid decision. I wanted to protect her. I wanted her to remain innocent and not think I would always be in danger. I wanted to protect her from yet another dead Dawkins brother."

"Trent... Honey..." His mother reached out and grabbed his hand.

"She's beyond furious, and she has a right to be."

"Have you tried to call her to explain?"

He shook his head. "No. Woof filled me in on everything she said to him about me and my stupidity. As soon as she found out I was going to be okay, she was furious."

"Yeah, that's how I found her. I get it now. But you have to realize she was hurting."

"I do. I get it. But I'm afraid the damage was extensive. And besides, I can't keep it from happening again. My job is dangerous. It's not fair to drag another person into my life. I'm afraid she wouldn't survive another dead fiancé."

His mother lifted his hand to her face and held it tight. "She's stronger than you give her credit for. And we don't choose who we fall in love with. When it happens, we just have to learn to live with all the shit that comes with loving someone, even if that shit includes the fact that one day that person might not come home to us."

"I hear your words, but you can't possibly step in my shoes."

His mother sat up straighter and shot him a strange glare. "I most certainly can, young man. My world wasn't perfect when I was your age, either. There are things about me I've never told you."

He frowned. *What the hell is she talking about*?

She took a breath and held his gaze. "You know my parents lived in Seattle, right?"

"Yes. You always told us that. When we were young, you said it was too far to visit them. When your father died, you went to the funeral alone and came home very sad. The only other time you went to visit was when your mother died. You were gone several days. I think Sean and I were about ten."

"That's right, and I was always surprised that your precocious mind didn't ask two thousand questions."

"Huh. You're right. That *is* strange. I don't know why. What happened?"

"They were filthy rich. That's what happened."

Trent winced. "Really?" He glanced around. "Where did all the money go?"

She chuckled, the most sardonic tone he'd ever heard from her. "It went to a potato farmer in Idaho."

"What?" Trent shifted, trying to sit up straighter.

She laughed a bit manically this time. "Yep. When I was eighteen, I came to Texas to go to college, wanting to spread my wings. I was raised with a silver spoon, and I wanted to know what it felt like to be a regular normal person. So, I lived frugally, created this whole other identity and met middle-class kids, including your father. We fell in love, and I put off telling him who I was because I didn't want him to reject me for lying to him. I was afraid and protecting myself. But when he proposed, I had to tell him the truth."

"Oh shit. You catfished him. Dad must have been pissed."

She lifted both brows. "That's an understatement. It wasn't that he cared about the money. It was that, in a way, I had lied to him. I knew my parents would never approve of him, but I cared more about William than I ever did my parents' stupid stock funds. We fought for weeks before I came to him and begged him to forgive me for my omission. I broke ties with my parents and never looked back. I've never been sorry, either. I'm pretty sure they gave that money to a farmer thinking it would infuriate me. The truth is, I was relieved. I didn't want to deal with it, ever."

"Wow. I can't believe you never told us that."

She shrugged. "I wasn't that girl anymore. I wanted you to have a middle-class life that included running around outside without worrying about getting your clothes dirty or needing to come inside for Latin lessons."

He cringed. "Latin?"

"I was completely fluent in that useless language when I graduated from high school."

He laughed.

She sobered. "Your father worried about my ability to give it all up for several years until we had a huge fight one day, and I told him he had to trust that I loved him enough to stay with him for the rest of my life without ever looking back."

"I'm so sorry. That must have been hard."

"It was. Harder for William than for me. I knew what I was giving up. I knew it was for the right reasons. I knew I would never, ever regret it."

"But he had to trust you."

"Exactly."

Trent groaned. "I'm you in this little tale."

She shrugged. "Sort of. In some ways, you're your father."

"I love her so much, Mom."

She squeezed his hand again. "I know you do. Just like I'm sure she loves you, too. But you have to trust that she can weather anything that happens. That your job will never be too much for her to handle. If you're not open with her, if you withhold the details, she will always worry she's not working with all the facts. In this case, those facts could have gotten her killed."

"That's why I didn't tell her."

His mother sighed. "Destiny isn't stupid, Trent. She knows exactly how dangerous your work is. After all, she already lost Sean to that danger. Her eyes are wide open. She knows there are aspects of your job you can't discuss. We all know that. But you left her in the dark intentionally about things that involved her. You did that to protect *you*; not her."

His mother was right.

She grabbed his hand and squeezed. "If Destiny's telling you she wants to be with you despite your job, and you keep her at arm's length to protect her, you're insulting her intelligence and treating her love like it's a fleeting thing."

Trent swallowed the giant lump in his throat and wiped his eyes again.

His mother stood, patted his arm, and kissed his forehead. She didn't say another word as she walked away, leaving him with his thoughts.

CHAPTER 27

Two weeks later…

"Destiny," Libby shouted from her bedroom. "Can you get the door? That's my date. I'm not ready."

"Sure." Destiny climbed off her bed, glanced down at her attire, and sighed. Normally, she would not greet Libby's dates wearing black leggings and an oversized Army T-shirt, but since he was already knocking, she couldn't help it. She adjusted the messy bun on top of her head and rushed down the stairs.

Catching a glimpse of herself in the mirror at the bottom of the stairs, she cringed. Yeah, she was a hot mess. The shirt was Trent's. He'd left it when he spent the night. She didn't even have on a bra. After four weeks without talking to him, texting him, or seeing him, she still spent most of her days off wallowing in self-pity alone in her room.

She'd cried too many times to count, and was in no way ready to go out with her girlfriends, let alone date.

By the time she reached the door, Libby's date had already knocked twice and rung the bell, so she didn't bother with the peephole; she simply yanked the door open.

And then she froze, her breath catching. "Trent..."

He was leaning hard on crutches under both arms, a giant, elaborate, black leg brace that extended from his hip to his ankle. Her eyes trailed upward to take in his loose sweatpants and a Delta Force T-shirt. He hadn't shaved in a few days, and his hair was the longest she'd seen it since they were kids.

She gripped the door so hard it was a wonder her fingers didn't hurt. "What are you doing here?"

"Could I maybe come in? It took me five minutes to get here from the car."

She yanked the door open wider, stepped completely out of the way, and let him pass. She had no idea what to say, but she obviously couldn't be a bitch to a man in a leg brace recovering from multiple gunshot wounds.

Wondering how the hell he'd gotten there, she peered outside, shocked to find his parents sitting in their SUV. "Your parents drove you here?"

"Yes. Don't worry. They're leaving," he tossed over his shoulder as he worked slowly toward her sofa. She noticed his duffel slung over his shoulder and that he carried a grocery bag. *What is he doing*?

Trent's parents waved at her and backed out of the spot. "I should go talk to them." It was the very last thing she wanted to do right now.

"Nope. You should shut the door and come talk to me."

She watched William and Nancy pull away and stepped back inside, shutting the door before she leaned against it. "Trent?"

He eased the duffel off his shoulder onto the floor and set the grocery bag on the coffee table, then dropped onto her sofa with a wince. He lifted his leg to extend it out straight on the cushions, taking up the entire sofa. "Mom and Dad have been wanting to spend a weekend in Dallas anyway, so they agreed to drop me off here."

"How did you know I would even be here?" She hadn't taken a step away from the door yet. It was holding her upright. *Damn, he looks good.* It was hard to remember she was furious with him and that he also hadn't contacted her in a month.

"I spoke to Libby," he informed her.

Destiny groaned as her shoulders sagged.

"She said you were off for three days. How did she get you to answer the door?" He was almost smirking. He was incredibly proud of himself, which played with her emotions.

"She said she had a date."

Libby came barreling down the stairs at that moment. "I might have lied." She had an overnight bag over her shoulder, and she came straight for the door. "I'm staying with Shayla and Bex for a few days." She stopped next to the couch and met Trent's gaze. "Don't forget. You owe me. I expect pictures of your hot friends in my inbox ASAP." She laughed.

Trent smirked at her. "How could I forget? I've got plenty of friends in mind."

Libby narrowed her eyes. "Do these friends have names? Or are you making them up?"

He shook his head. "I would never make something like that up. I've got a mental list going. Hatch, Kraft, Tank, Sweets..."

"Please tell me those are nicknames."

He nodded.

"Thank God." Before Destiny could respond, Libby turned and rushed past Destiny and out the front door.

Traitor.

Destiny returned her gaze to Trent. "You're going to stay here?"

"Yes. I know it's presumptuous, but it was the only way I could think of to get you to see me and prevent you from being able to escape."

She crossed her arms. "A bit upper-handed don't you think?"

"Yep. There is no other way to describe it."

"What if I don't want you to stay here?"

"Tough. I'm not leaving. I figured it might take me three days of groveling to get you back on my good side, so I made sure I would have all seventy-two hours to plead my case." He leaned over and picked up the bag from the coffee table. The first thing he pulled out was a single red rose. The second item was a small box of chocolates. He held both out toward her. "I told you once I wasn't a roses and chocolates kind of guy. I changed my mind."

She rolled her eyes. "You can't buy my forgiveness, Trent."

"I know that, but I thought it was a good start." He set the two items on the table and licked his lips. "I have a speech too. You want to hear it?"

She almost smiled, pissed with herself for being weak. She was supposed to be mad at him. "You could have called."

"Would you have answered?"

"No."

He lifted both brows.

Finally, she sighed and shuffled toward him, dropping into the armchair that sat at an angle to the sofa. "You hurt me."

"I know, Des." When he said her name in that tone reserved only for him, she melted a little.

She drew her legs up and wrapped her arms around her shins, setting her chin on her knees.

"I made bad choices. I'm so sorry. In my stupid mind, I thought I was doing the right thing, protecting you."

"You made me feel like it was you who didn't want anyone to know we were dating, Trent. I was confused. And then you were cryptic and distant and basically lying to me. Why? I'm not a fragile butterfly. You know that. I could have handled the truth, but you didn't trust me to be strong enough to deal with the fact that there was a threat to your life."

"You're right." He held her gaze.

She lifted her chin a few inches. "That's all you have to say? I'm right?"

"Not even close." He took a deep breath. "My mom told me this long, convoluted story about when she met my dad, an interesting story I'll tell you later. Anyway, she made me realize I was keeping secrets from you to protect myself more than you."

Destiny narrowed her eyes. *What is he talking about?*

"I was scared. Afraid you would leave me if you knew how damn dangerous my job could be. In truth, something like this never happens. We go on a mission, protect someone, rescue someone, hide someone. Even when we've had to kill to do that, it doesn't blow back on us."

"Except this time, it did."

"Yes. In a big way. I couldn't see a way out. In no scenario I made up in my head was I ever going to be able to walk freely in public again in my life. There was a lot of crazy shit going on in my mind. I was afraid I'd be killed and you'd be left to deal with another Dawkins funeral. I was afraid something would happen to you because of me. If the fucker tracking me had found you..." He cringed.

"Trent..."

He continued. "I also selfishly didn't want you to leave me if you found out how high the stakes were. I couldn't blame you. It was too much to ask of anyone."

"Except you *didn't* ask, Trent. You made the decision for me."

"Yeah. It wasn't fair. I see that now."

"It wasn't even kind of fair. You don't get to make choices for me. You don't get a say in what I can and can't handle. I'm a grown woman. If I want to enter into a committed relationship with a dedicated member of Delta Force, then I get to make that choice on my own. If I fall in love with such a man, then I get to decide if it's worth it to me or not. You don't get a say in it." Suddenly, she felt like she sounded ridiculous.

"Are you?" Trent asked.

"Am I what?"

"In love with such a man."

She licked her lips, a tear sliding down her face which she swiped away. "Yes."

"Is he worth it?"

She hesitated. How had he managed to barge into her condo, announce he was going to stay three days, and then win her over with his apology in less than ten minutes?

"Des..." His voice was deep, gravelly. He reached out a hand. "Come here."

She took several shallow breaths, staring at his outstretched hand before she dropped her feet to the floor, shoved from the chair, and closed the distance. The moment she was close enough, he grabbed her hand and tugged her. She didn't want to hurt his leg, so she sat on the floor next to him. One palm smoothed around her neck, his fingers threading in the messy bun. "I want to be worth all the hardship I bring to your door. I want to be someone you love no matter what. Someone you trust to protect you. I want to be that man. Please forgive me."

She wiped away the stupid tears again, noticing he had a few of his own shimmering in his eyes.

"I often can't give you much information about a

mission, but I promise I will never leave you in the dark like that again. I will trust that you can handle it. I will remind myself that in your eyes I'm worth it and that nothing will spook you into leaving me."

She nodded, crying now.

He urged her forward with the hand on her head until their faces were closer. His other hand went to her waist. "Nice shirt."

A short chuckle escaped her as he lightened the moment. "Some guy left it here. It smelled like him for several weeks. I'm gonna need him to wear it again to reinforce the scent."

"Is he worth it?"

"Yes. He's worth it. And so much more."

"I love you, Destiny."

"I love you too, Trent."

He pulled her in the last few inches and kissed her, a slow, gentle kiss that sent a shiver down her spine and made her toes curl. When he finally parted from her, he let out a deep breath. "Thank God you didn't turn me down because I feared if I couldn't convince you to take me back, I would be left lying here for three days without food or a shower or any kind of assistance. I'm kinda needy for a few more weeks," he joked.

"Big, tough Delta guy? You're anything but needy," she joked back. She glanced down at his leg. "Does it hurt?"

"Not much." He rubbed his chest. "You missed the giant purple bruise on my chest. Oh, and my eardrum has started healing enough that I'm no longer underwater. That just leaves my leg. I need a few months of physical therapy before I can go back to work. I could use a new nurse. I'm growing tired of my mom."

Destiny rolled her eyes again. "So, you came here because you needed me to cook for you and give you sponge baths?"

He lifted one brow, smirking. "I like the sound of the sponge baths."

She swatted at his arm.

"Nah. I can take the brace off to shower. Oh, and I have a new scar next to the first one. It's not quite as jagged, but I'm hoping the guys don't rename me Double Zip or something equally annoying."

She giggled. "You realize if you aren't a good patient, I could make a suggestion like that, and your life would be miserable."

He tugged her hair. "You wouldn't."

"Try me."

Destiny held his gaze for several moments, enjoying the way he looked at her. "Speaking of nicknames, I didn't recognize that list you rattled off to Libby. I know Jangles, Woof, Merlin, and Duff. Those were not among the names you gave Libby. Did you make them up on the spot?" She was half-kidding, but Libby would kill him with her bare hands if he pulled her chain.

Trent cupped her face. "No, I did not make them up. They're other guys I know from the Army. All of them are legit. I promise."

She eyes him wearily. "Kraft? Like the mac and cheese? That sounds made up."

He laughed. "Nope. That's what we call him, and yes,

like the mac and cheese. But I think Libby might like my friend Jason Nixon. Hatch. He's not in town right now, but I'll show him a picture of her when I see him."

Destiny groaned. "This plan sounds like it could go south in a hurry."

"Hey, I'm not forcing anyone's hand. You're the one with friends who have glassy eyes for military men."

Destiny leaned in and set her forehead against Trent's. She didn't want to think about Libby or any of her other friends right now. She wanted to focus on the man in front of her who'd stolen her heart.

CHAPTER 28

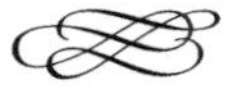

Two weeks later...

Destiny set a pillow under Trent's ankle, propping it up on her grandmother's coffee table. The woman had done nothing but grin since they'd arrived fifteen minutes ago. She nearly bounced as she took a seat. "Other than the brace, you look good, Trent," she told him.

"Thank you, Stella." He'd called her by her first name at her insistence his entire life, even before Destiny had moved in.

"To what do I owe this visit?"

Trent reached out and clasped Destiny's hand, pulling her down to sit next to him.

Destiny was perplexed and a bit nervous about this visit. She had taken a leave of absence from her job for one month so she could come to Killeen with Trent and help him out while he healed. That was kind of an excuse really, and they both knew it. It was the story she told her boss. The truth was, Trent could get around fine on his own. He wasn't fast, but he didn't need constant help or supervision.

The real reason she'd taken the time off was to be with him. They'd agreed it would be nearly impossible to be certain of their path together without seeing each other slightly more than one night every few weeks. Destiny hadn't needed even one day. She'd been sure about Trent for over a decade. She doubted he'd needed the time to solidify his feelings, either.

But God, it felt nice to be able to spend every single day with him. They came back to his apartment after just one night in hers so he wouldn't have to navigate her stairs. This way, they were also closer to his team and his parents, all of whom had stopped by to visit—at least one of them making an appearance every day. Luckily, none of them stayed for more than an hour because Destiny hadn't been in the mood to share him for longer than that.

Trent had woken up this morning, taken a phone call, and then grown sober. She'd figured his call had been work-related, so she hadn't asked any questions. Therefore, it shocked her when he insisted they needed to come see Stella this morning, and then they would go visit his parents.

Trent squeezed her hand, scaring her. If he weren't so serious, she would've thought he intended to propose or something, but his demeanor wasn't right for that. "I need to tell you both something."

"Okay," Stella murmured.

"Trent?" Destiny stared at him, watching him breathe a bit heavily.

He glanced at her grandma and then back at her. "I did something without consulting you first."

Destiny flinched. "What do you mean?"

"Several weeks ago, even before my accident, I sent a lock of your hair to have a DNA test done."

Destiny frowned. "What for?" Then she gasped. "My mother…" She remembered him telling her there was a possibility he could find a match.

He nodded and glanced at her grandmother. "I wouldn't have said anything if there hadn't been a match, but I knew if I could prove anything, it would give you both some peace."

Destiny licked her lips. "She's dead?"

Trent nodded. "Yes. I'm so sorry." He squeezed her hand, pulled her into his side, and then shifted his gaze to her grandmother. "I know this is difficult to hear."

Her grandma nodded slowly. "I guess in my heart I always knew. That's why I stopped looking for her. It was like a maternal instinct or something. I just knew. Where's her body?"

"She was found dead from an overdose, probably the same day she never returned home. Without ID and because of her location, all the coroner could do was run a DNA test and file the information for a possible future match. She was cremated, and her remains are buried in an unidentified plot. We can go there if you want to sometime."

Her grandma nodded and forced a smile. "I'd like that."

Trent hugged Destiny close to his side and kissed the top of her head. "I'm so sorry, Des. I hope you're not mad."

She shook her head. Truthfully, all she felt was relieved. At least now she knew. She lifted her gaze. "Was there any match to my father?"

"No. But that means very little. Remember, I told you, if we found a match, we would know. If we didn't find anything, that doesn't mean he's not alive. It just means no one cataloged his DNA results."

Destiny nodded. She doubted he'd ever known she existed.

"If he, or anyone in his immediate family, ever runs a test through one of the main ancestry systems, you could get a match. But right now, the only close relative that shows up for you is Stella."

Destiny nodded again, slightly numb. It was kind of sad and lonely knowing that she had no living relatives besides her grandmother.

Stella cleared her throat. "Hey, DNA isn't always the best indicator of family. You have an amazing family that loves you to pieces if you count Nancy and William."

"And me," Trent pointed out. "And…if you wanted to increase the list of immediate family for possible emergency contacts for work or something, you could always marry me."

Destiny blinked at him, her mind backing up, trying to figure out what he'd just said.

Her grandmother gasped and then clapped her hands together.

"Did you just propose to me?"

Trent scrunched up his nose. "I guess I did. I didn't mean to blurt it out right now exactly, two minutes after telling you your mother died, but you just looked so forlorn and I couldn't help myself."

Destiny shoved off him and sat up straighter. "That was the corniest proposal I've ever heard."

"I think it was perfectly romantic," her grandmother stated with a giggle. "Answer the man."

Destiny drew back, shooting him a narrowed gaze. "I don't think he technically asked me a question." Her heart was racing. She'd been with him only two weeks, plus a few random dates before that. *Isn't it a bit soon to get engaged?* She shook the thought from her mind. She'd dreamed of marrying Trent for half her life.

Trent leaned to one side and reached behind him. A second later, he held a small box out in front of her. "Destiny Fisher, will you marry me?"

She clapped a hand over her mouth, her eyes wide. "You planned this?"

"Of course. I mean, I didn't mean to do it right this second. I was picturing something slightly more romantic, maybe on my parents' porch swing later today or something. But then that cheesy line slipped out. I guess I couldn't wait." He grinned. "You still haven't answered me."

"Yes," she shouted as she threw her arms around his neck. Thank God she no longer needed to be gentle with his ear or his chest because she couldn't have stopped herself. His bulky leg brace kept her from getting any closer, but she managed to flatten herself to his front as best as possible.

When she finally released him, he kissed her gently and then slid the ring onto her finger.

She stared at it, holding her hand in front of her eyes. A delicate gold band with a solitaire. Simple. Perfect. Exactly right. "I love it," she whispered, wiggling her fingers and then shifting her hand so that her grandmother could see.

"You two better go next door and tell your parents. They'll feel left out if they find out you got engaged and kept it from them for hours," her grandmother teased.

Trent groaned. "Can't we just have a few more minutes before my mom starts planning the wedding of the century?"

Destiny pinched his arm playfully. "Don't be mean. Let your mom plan. You know I don't care about that sort of thing. All I care about is being with you. If it makes her happy to organize a huge production, you keep your mouth shut."

Trent pursed his lips and then grinned. "Yes, ma'am."

God, I love this man. His eyes danced with the same emotion she felt. As they stared at each other, Stella quietly eased from the room.

Trent threaded his hand in her hair and hauled her mouth closer again. "I love you so much, Des," he whispered against her lips.

"I love you, too." She kissed him, twisting around to face him better, longing for the day when he wouldn't need this brace anymore. The damn thing hadn't kept them from getting creative in the last week and figuring out all sorts of ways to have sex without reinjuring his leg, but she would still be giddy when he didn't need to be quite so careful anymore. She flattened a hand on his chest. "We should go tell your parents."

He closed his eyes. "Give me one more minute of peace with my woman, please." He ran his hand up and down her back.

"Come on. You're overreacting. It won't be that bad. At least she knows we're together now. We aren't going to blindside her."

"I'll bet you a homemade supreme pizza that she has a Pinterest page and a binder already started."

"How are you going to cook a pizza with that leg, Trent?" she teased.

"I'm not. I know my mom. I'll win. And you know her, too. Hell, you've been through this with my mom before." He sobered as he spoke those words.

Destiny cupped his face. "I miss him, too. I wish he could be here. I know he'd be happy for us."

Trent nodded. "I know that, too." He lifted her hand and kissed her fingers, rubbing the ring against his lips. "Sometimes I can feel him, and I always get a sense of peace. It's like I know he's smiling down at us. It's what he wanted."

Destiny held Trent very close, wrapping her hand around the back of his neck. "I get that now. We're going to be the cheesiest couple of everyone we know."

Trent chuckled. "That's the truth. Already handed my man card to Woof yesterday when he came by. He rolled his eyes every time you walked by me and reached out to touch me."

Destiny smiled wider. "You don't even care."

"Nope. They can tease me all they want. Joke's on them." He kissed her fingers again and stared down at the ring. "The prize is all mine."

Destiny couldn't even respond to that. She knew in her heart she was the winner here. But it wasn't a contest. Trent loved her just as fiercely as she loved him. He showed her in a dozen ways every single day. She would never take it for granted. And she wouldn't waste a single moment they spent together feeling insecure for the rest of their lives.

Life was short. Love was precious.

Time was a gift.

Please enjoy the following excerpt from *Gwen's Delta* by Lynne St. James.

Luke "Merlin" Forest turned off into a parking spot in front of Camelot Rare Books and Antiquities and shut off the engine of his truck. Bone-deep exhaustion covered him like a warm blanket, and he leaned against the headrest and ran his hand through his hair. The guys ribbed him for the grey at his temples, making him look older than thirty-five. Though not as old as he felt. He'd wanted to hug his CO when he announced they had a week off. It couldn't have come at a better time.

It was ages since he'd been in a bookstore and even longer since he'd been in one that sold old and out-of-print editions. Rare books were his weakness, one he hadn't shared with many people, including his teammates. They already thought he was too quiet and a little weird.

As Merlin stepped inside, he was enveloped in the scent of old books, instantly transported back to an easier time as a child, wandering through the bookshelves with his grandfather. It was hard to believe he'd ever been that idealistic, so convinced he could save the world.

"I'll be right with you." The woman's Southern drawl sounded more sultry than sweet as she focused on the computer in front of her. He couldn't see her face. The fall of her auburn hair blocked his view.

"Thank you. But if it's okay, I'll just take a look around."

"Of course." She looked up from the computer screen. "Oh, I'm sorry. I thought you were someone else."

As he met her gaze, he sucked in a breath. Her emerald green eyes glowed against her fair skin. When she smiled, her face lit up and ignited a fire that raced down his spine, rooting him to the floor like he'd been struck by lightning.

"Are you okay?" she asked gently.

"Yeah, I'm fine. Just uh...letting my vision adjust from outside," Merlin replied.

Holy shit. One smile from a beautiful woman and he couldn't put words together and got an instant hard-on like he was fifteen.

"Okay. Let me know if you need help with anything," she said with another killer smile.

What the hell just happened? He'd never reacted like

that to a woman. The soft echo of her voice sounded in his head; he wanted to hear more of it. Small talk wasn't his thing. Neither was dating. He'd decided long ago that the Army was his focus, and there wasn't room for the distraction of family. After seeing how Woof's and Zip's concern for their women changed their focus, it only increased his resolve.

Until now.

Ducking out of view, he focused on the book titles, anything to distract him from her eyes and lips. *Damn.* This wasn't helping the erection straining against his zipper.

As he contemplated whether he should leave, the murmur of voices back up front caught his attention. They were too low for him to make out from where he stood, so he walked deeper into the stacks. He should feel guilty for listening, but it was a public place with no guarantee of privacy. At least, that's what he told himself.

"Here, sweetie, you work too hard." The voice sounded like an older woman.

"Thanks, Grams. You make the best lemonade."

If he remembered correctly, the store was owned by a family. Was this redhead the granddaughter?

"You think compliments will get me to leave you alone? You need more of a life than this store, Gwen."

"You can't fault a girl for trying," the redhead replied with a giggle.

"What am I going to do with you?"

"Same thing you always do—shake your head and go bake."

He struggled to stifle his chuckle. Their relationship was close and reminded him of his granddad.

Listening to their conversation, hearing their love, opened a hole in his heart he'd kept patched for years. The need to learn more about her was irresistible.

Merlin didn't want to startle them, so he approached the desk slowly. When he stopped in front of them, the women turned his way.

As he drew closer, the redhead's floral scent mixed with the old book smell. Freckles spread across her nose and cheeks and added to his attraction. It was soft, delicate, and now, unforgettable.

"Did you find something?" she asked.

"Yes. No. I mean…umm… I'm not sure. I've been looking for an old first edition, one of my unicorns."

Stuttering? What the hell is wrong with me? This woman was dangerous to his equilibrium. He should have brought one of the guys as their whining about being in a bookstore would have kept his head on straight.

It took all his willpower not to reach out and push an auburn lock behind her ear. Was it as soft as it looked?

"Well, if we don't have it here, we can try to locate a copy for you," Gwen replied.

"Why don't you take a break? You can take this nice man for coffee," the older woman said with a smile.

"Grams, *geesh*. Not too subtle." She turned back to him. "I'm so sorry. You'll have to excuse my grandmother. I think she's getting senile in her old age." A light, peachy-pink color infused her cheeks.

His heart flipped over in his chest. Coffee with Gwen sounded like a wonderful idea. The name fit her —gentle and lovely.

"I don't know. I can always go for a cup of coffee or four. I'm Merlin, by the way." He smiled, hoping she'd agree to the impromptu date.

Her grandmother smiled. "See, he wants coffee. And you can talk about books. Is this your first time here, Merlin?"

"Yes, it is. I recently moved to the area." Since Gwen still hadn't answered, he added, "I promise I don't bite, unless you ask, that is." Merlin waggled his eyebrows. He hoped she'd laugh again.

"Neither of you will give up until I say yes, so I don't have much choice. But there will be no biting on the first date," Gwen answered with a smile and her eyes sparkled with mischief.

He was toast...

*

Be sure to pick up the next book book in the Delta Team Three series, Gwen's Delta by Lynne St. James.

AUTHOR'S NOTE

I hope you've enjoyed *Destiny's Delta*! If you haven't read the rest of the books in the series, I've included the links for all five stories.

Nori's Delta by Lori Ryan
Destiny's Delta by Becca Jameson
Gwen's Delta by Lynne St. James
Ivy's Delta by Elle James
Hope's Delta by Riley Edwards

You may have also noticed that *Destiny's Delta* is the launching pad for my next series, **Open Skies**! Yep, all those flight attendants you met have their own happily ever afters with their own sexy Deltas.

Open Skies:
Layover
Redeye
Nonstop

Standby

I'm including the first chapter of *Layover* to whet your appetite! Mwahaha

"That one," Libby whispered as she set her elbows on the high-top table where the two women stood and leaned in closer to Christa, her breath hitching.

Christa glanced at Libby and then followed her line of sight. "The tall one?"

"They're all tall. You think it's a requirement or something?" she joked, sitting up straighter. "Maybe there's a height requirement for men who enter the military."

Christa rolled her pale blue eyes and tucked a lock of blond hair behind her ear. "There is no height requirement for the military."

Libby shot her a goofy glance. "I was kidding."

"You're not wrong though. It seems like all of Trent's friends are tall. And built. And…do these guys ever eat junk food?"

The man Libby had her sights on glanced their direction. When he turned his body, she licked her lips. He had on khaki dress pants, a pale-blue, button-down shirt, and loafers. Casual but stylish. Like the rest of the wedding party at Destiny and Trent's rehearsal dinner.

Libby smiled at him. And then she melted a bit when he returned the smile.

Christa jerked her gaze downward and muttered, "Shit. He caught us ogling."

"Ogling? We're downright staring, and I don't care if he did catch us. Me in particular. I hope he's single."

Christa lifted her gaze back to face Libby. Her cheeks were pink, which happened often considering how pale Christa's skin was and how easily she embarrassed. "Does it even matter? If all you care about is a one-night stand with one of these guys, what difference does it make if he's single or not?"

Libby gasped in mock horror. "I'm not stealing some other woman's man." Destiny, one of her best friends and the star of this weekend, hadn't mentioned any of her fiancé Trent's friends being married or even in serious relationships. So Libby wasn't too worried. She was on a mission. Her goal for the night was to choose a willing, handsome, buff guy and then flirt mercilessly with him.

Tomorrow night was when she intended to strike, after the wedding itself. Tonight would be too obvious in this more intimate gathering in the reserved room at the back of an Italian restaurant. Besides, it would be awkward tomorrow if she slept with one of the groomsmen and then had to face him at the wedding.

She was pretty sure the man she'd singled out who was now glancing at her yet again was named Jason Nixon. It was nearly impossible to keep up with any one of Trent's friend's names since half the time he called them by their last name, and the other half of the time he referred to them by their team nickname. But she'd heard them refer to this tall, broad, breath of fresh air as Hatch.

"I don't know how you can possibly set your mind to

having sex with a stranger before you've even met him," Christa continued, her voice low, her eyes darting around as if the mention of the word sex might cause eyebrows to rise.

"Girl, do you have any idea what kind of men I've dated? I'm twenty-eight years old. My mother has set me up with half the Guatemalan men anywhere close to my age in a thirty-mile radius. Every one of them has been a failure."

Christa giggled. "Your mom *is* persistent."

"That's an understatement. She doesn't seem to grasp that since I was born and raised in Dallas, I spent my life exposed to a far more diverse culture than she's from." Libby glanced at Christa. "The guys she sets me up with are always cocky and macho. They may act perfectly polite when they're around my parents, but as soon as we're alone it's like they puff out their chests and start some sort of mating dance." Libby shuddered at the reminder.

Christa laughed harder. "Don't forget, I've been with you on a few double dates. I've seen this mating dance in action. Your description is hilarious but spot-on."

Libby sighed as she glanced again at Jason. "I want to know what it feels like to be with a man who's more interested in me than himself. That guy..." She nodded once again toward the man who'd grabbed her attention, "...makes me squirm. I like the way he smiles at me. It doesn't hurt that he's rock hard, muscular, and tall." Libby sighed dramatically.

"Not gonna lie. He looks pretty cocky himself."

Libby shook her head. "No. It's different. He looks

confident. Alpha, but not in a macho sort of way," she mused. "I've always had a bit of a thing for men in uniform. I'm dying to roll around between the sheets with one of them."

"And you think if you sleep with one of these guys, you'll get it out of your system? Seems like a risky idea."

Libby nodded. "That's my plan."

"What are you going to tell your mom when you end up falling for him?"

Libby cringed. "Not gonna happen. My parents would have a coronary if I dated a man like that cool drink of water. He has so many strikes against him, she'd drop dead. He's full-blooded American for one thing, and white."

"Might I remind you that you're full-blooded American too," Christa pointed out. "It's not a race."

Libby laughed. "To my mother it is. 'Guatemalans must stick together,'" she began in her mother's authoritative tone. 'It's time for you to find a nice man from our country and settle down. I'm not getting any younger. I need grandbabies.'"

Christa winced. "Yeah, your mom does kinda sound like that."

"And the crazy thing is that she was born in the US too. I guess the fact that she lived in a less diverse community growing up caused her to absorb more of the traditional Guatemalan ways of thinking. I thought maybe she would lighten up after her parents passed away, but noooo. If anything, she lays it on even thicker."

"Shit. He's coming this way," Christa whispered.

Libby sat up straighter, smoothing her hands down her dress, over her thighs. She hoped her makeup looked okay. She hadn't reapplied lipstick since they'd finished dinner.

Suddenly, she felt a bit silly and presumptuous. It wasn't like her to pick out a man from across a room and set her sights on him. She honestly hadn't dated many white guys, and none as formidable as this one.

His gaze was definitely set on her as he approached, his swagger slightly cocky, his lips tipped up almost in a smirk. Maybe he was no different than the macho guys she was used to, but somehow he had a different vibe. Her body had come alive more and more throughout the evening. By now, she was buzzing with arousal. Most of the men she'd dated made her cringe and shrink away from them within minutes. Not this one. By the time he reached their table, Libby was no longer breathing. She had to tip her head way back to meet his gaze.

He turned toward Christa. "I haven't had a chance to meet you two yet." He held out a hand. "Jason Nixon."

At least Libby had his name right in her head.

Christa shook his hand in her small pale one, barely managing to murmur, "Christa Boyce." She took a step back, pointing over her shoulder. "I'm just gonna go get a drink." She fled so fast it was a wonder a breeze didn't hit Libby in the face.

Jason turned his attention toward Libby once again and took her hand next. "And you are?"

"Libby. Libby Garcia," she stammered, loving the feel of his firm handshake. His hand was darn near twice the size of hers. Granted, everything about her was petite. She was four eleven and proportionately dainty. Most of the time that fact drove her crazy, and she worked hard to make up for her size with personality. With Jason, she suddenly didn't mind. He seemed huge and powerful, and she liked it.

"Libby. Is that short for Elizabeth?"

She shook her head and cleared her throat. "No. Libertad."

"Ah, Hispanic. Libertad. Liberty. I love that." His accent was nearly perfect.

Her eyes widened. For one thing, no one ever loved her weird name. And for another thing, Jason Nixon apparently spoke at least enough Spanish to correctly pronounce and translate Liberty. *Interesting*. "Thank you," she managed to murmur as he released her fingers.

"Nice to meet you, Libby. Save a dance for me tomorrow night?"

She nearly choked as she stared at his raised eyebrow. She was not going to chicken out. She was so totally going to lay it on thick with this hunk. "Absolutely. Looking forward to it."

If you'd like to read more, here is the link for *Layover*, Open Skies, Book One.

ALSO BY BECCA JAMESON

Open Skies:

Layover

Redeye

Nonstop

Standby

Canyon Springs:

Caleb's Mate

Hunter's Mate

Corked and Tapped:

Volume One: Friday Night

Volume Two: Company Party

Volume Three: The Holidays

Surrender:

Raising Lucy

Teaching Abby

Leaving Roman

Choosing Kellen

Pleasing Josie

Project DEEP:

Reviving Emily

Reviving Trish

Reviving Dade

Reviving Zeke

Reviving Graham

Reviving Bianca

Reviving Olivia

Project DEEP Box Set One

Project DEEP Box Set Two

SEALs in Paradise:

Hot SEAL, Red Wine

Hot SEAL, Australian Nights

Hot SEAL, Cold Feet

Dark Falls:

Dark Nightmares

Club Zodiac:

Training Sasha

Obeying Rowen

Collaring Brooke

Mastering Rayne

Trusting Aaron

Claiming London

Sharing Charlotte

Taming Rex

Tempting Elizabeth

Club Zodiac Box Set One

Club Zodiac Box Set Two

The Art of Kink:

Pose

Paint

Sculpt

Arcadian Bears:

Grizzly Mountain

Grizzly Beginning

Grizzly Secret

Grizzly Promise

Grizzly Survival

Grizzly Perfection

Arcadian Bears Box Set One

Arcadian Bears Box Set Two

Sleeper SEALs:

Saving Zola

Spring Training:

Catching Zia

Catching Lily

Catching Ava

Spring Training Box Set

The Underground series:

Force

Clinch

Guard

Submit

Thrust

Torque

The Underground Box Set One

The Underground Box Set Two

Saving Sofia (Special Forces: Operations Alpha)

Wolf Masters series:

Kara's Wolves

Lindsey's Wolves

Jessica's Wolves

Alyssa's Wolves

Tessa's Wolf

Rebecca's Wolves

Melinda's Wolves

Laurie's Wolves

Amanda's Wolves

Sharon's Wolves

Wolf Masters Box Set One

Wolf Masters Box Set Two

Claiming Her series:

The Rules

The Game

The Prize

Emergence series:

Bound to be Taken

Bound to be Tamed

Bound to be Tested

Bound to be Tempted

Emergence Box Set

The Fight Club series:

Come

Perv

Need

Hers

Want

Lust

The Fight Club Box Set One

The Fight Club Box Set Two

Wolf Gatherings series:

Tarnished

Dominated

Completed

Redeemed

Abandoned

Betrayed

Wolf Gatherings Box Set One

Wolf Gathering Box Set Two

Durham Wolves series:

Rescue in the Smokies

Fire in the Smokies

Freedom in the Smokies

Stand Alone Books:

Blind with Love

Guarding the Truth

Out of the Smoke

Abducting His Mate

Three's a Cruise

Wolf Trinity

Frostbitten

A Princess for Cale/A Princess for Cain

ABOUT THE AUTHOR

Becca Jameson is a USA Today best-selling author of over 100 books. She is well-known for her Wolf Masters series, her Fight Club series, and her Club Zodiac series. She currently lives in Houston, Texas, with her husband and her Goldendoodle. Two grown kids pop in every once in a while too! She is loving this journey and has dabbled in a variety of genres, including paranormal, sports romance, military, and BDSM.

A total night owl, Becca writes late at night, sequestering herself in her office with a glass of red wine and a bar of dark chocolate, her fingers flying across the keyboard as her characters weave their own stories.

During the day--which never starts before ten in the morning!--she can be found jogging, running errands, or reading in her favorite hammock chair!

...where Alphas dominate...

Becca's Newsletter Sign-up

Join my Facebook fan group, Becca's Bibliomaniacs, for the most up-to-date information, random excerpts while I work, giveaways, and fun release parties!

Facebook Fan Group:
Becca's Bibliomaniacs

Contact Becca:
www.beccajameson.com
beccajameson4@aol.com

facebook.com/becca.jameson.18
twitter.com/beccajameson
instagram.com/becca.jameson
bookbub.com/authors/becca-jameson
goodreads.com/beccajameson
amazon.com/author/beccajameson

There are many more books in this fan fiction world than listed here, for an up-to-date list go to www.AcesPress.com

Special Forces: Operation Alpha World

Christie Adams: Charity's Heart
Denise Agnew: Dangerous to Hold
Shauna Allen: Awakening Aubrey
Brynne Asher: Blackburn
Linzi Baxter: Unlocking Dreams
Jennifer Becker: Hiding Catherine
Alice Bello: Shadowing Milly
Heather Blair: Rescue Me
Anna Blakely: Rescuing Gracelynn
Julia Bright: Saving Lorelei
Cara Carnes: Protecting Mari
Kendra Mei Chailyn: Beast
Melissa Kay Clarke: Rescuing Annabeth
Samantha A. Cole: Handling Haven
Sue Coletta: Hacked
Melissa Combs: Gallant
Anne Conley: Redemption for Misty
KaLyn Cooper: Rescuing Melina
Janie Crouch: Storm
Liz Crowe: Marking Mariah
Sarah Curtis: Securing the Odds
Jordan Dane: Redemption for Avery
Tarina Deaton: Found in the Lost
Aspen Drake, Intense
KL Donn: Unraveling Love
Riley Edwards: Protecting Olivia

PJ Fiala: Defending Sophie
Nicole Flockton: Protecting Maria
Michele Gwynn: Rescuing Emma
Casey Hagen: Shielding Nebraska
Desiree Holt: Protecting Maddie
Kathy Ivan: Saving Sarah
Kris Jacen, Be With Me
Jesse Jacobson: Protecting Honor
Silver James: Rescue Moon
Becca Jameson: Saving Sofia
Kate Kinsley: Protecting Ava
Heather Long: Securing Arizona
Gennita Low: No Protection
Kirsten Lynn: Joining Forces for Jesse
Margaret Madigan: Bang for the Buck
Kimberly McGath: The Predecessor
Rachel McNeely: The SEAL's Surprise Baby
KD Michaels: Saving Laura
Lynn Michaels, Rescuing Kyle
Wren Michaels: The Fox & The Hound
Kat Mizera: Protecting Bobbi
Keira Montclair, Wolf and the Wild Scots
Mary B Moore: Force Protection
LeTeisha Newton: Protecting Butterfly
Angela Nicole: Protecting the Donna
MJ Nightingale: Protecting Beauty
Sarah O'Rourke: Saving Liberty
Victoria Paige: Reclaiming Izabel
Anne L. Parks: Mason
Debra Parmley: Protecting Pippa
Lainey Reese: Protecting New York

TL Reeve and Michele Ryan: Extracting Mateo
Elena M. Reyes: Keeping Ava
Angela Rush: Charlotte
Rose Smith: Saving Satin
Jenika Snow: Protecting Lily
Lynne St. James: SEAL's Spitfire
Dee Stewart: Conner
Harley Stone: Rescuing Mercy
Jen Talty: Burning Desire
Reina Torres, Rescuing Hi'ilani
Savvi V: Loving Lex
Megan Vernon: Protecting Us
Rachel Young: Because of Marissa

Delta Team Three Series

Lori Ryan: Nori's Delta
Becca Jameson: Destiny's Delta
Lynne St James, Gwen's Delta
Elle James: Ivy's Delta
Riley Edwards: Hope's Delta

Police and Fire: Operation Alpha World

Freya Barker: Burning for Autumn
B.P. Beth: Scott
Jane Blythe: Salvaging Marigold
Julia Bright, Justice for Amber
Anna Brooks, Guarding Georgia
KaLyn Cooper: Justice for Gwen
Aspen Drake: Sheltering Emma
Deanndra Hall: Shelter for Sharla
Barb Han: Kace

EM Hayes: Gambling for Ashleigh
CM Steele: Guarding Hope
Reina Torres: Justice for Sloane
Aubree Valentine, Justice for Danielle
Maddie Wade: Finding English
Stacey Wilk: Stage Fright
Laine Vess: Justice for Lauren

Tarpley VFD Series

Silver James, Fighting for Elena
Deanndra Hall, Fighting for Carly
Haven Rose, Fighting for Calliope
MJ Nightingale, Fighting for Jemma
TL Reeve, Fighting for Brittney
Nicole Flockton, Fighting for Nadia

As you know, this book included at least one character from Susan Stoker's books. To check out more, see below.

SEAL of Protection: Legacy Series

Securing Caite
Securing Brenae (novella)
Securing Sidney
Securing Piper
Securing Zoey
Securing Avery
Securing Kalee (Sept 2020)
Securing Jane (Feb 2021)

SEAL Team Hawaii Series

Finding Elodie (Apr 2021)
Finding Lexie (Aug 2021)
Finding Kenna (Oct 2021)
Finding Monica (TBA)
Finding Carly (TBA)
Finding Ashlyn (TBA)

Delta Team Two Series

Shielding Gillian
Shielding Kinley
Shielding Aspen (Oct 2020)
Shielding Riley (Jan 2021)
Shielding Devyn (May 2021)
Shielding Ember (Sep 2021)
Shielding Sierra (TBA)

Delta Force Heroes Series

Rescuing Rayne (FREE!)
Rescuing Aimee (novella)
Rescuing Emily
Rescuing Harley
Marrying Emily (novella)
Rescuing Kassie
Rescuing Bryn
Rescuing Casey
Rescuing Sadie (novella)
Rescuing Wendy
Rescuing Mary
Rescuing Macie (Novella)

Badge of Honor: Texas Heroes Series

Justice for Mackenzie (FREE!)
Justice for Mickie
Justice for Corrie
Justice for Laine (novella)
Shelter for Elizabeth
Justice for Boone
Shelter for Adeline
Shelter for Sophie
Justice for Erin
Justice for Milena
Shelter for Blythe
Justice for Hope
Shelter for Quinn
Shelter for Koren
Shelter for Penelope

SEAL of Protection Series

Protecting Caroline (FREE!)
Protecting Alabama
Protecting Fiona
Marrying Caroline (novella)
Protecting Summer
Protecting Cheyenne
Protecting Jessyka
Protecting Julie (novella)
Protecting Melody
Protecting the Future
Protecting Kiera (novella)
Protecting Alabama's Kids (novella)
Protecting Dakota

New York Times, USA Today and *Wall Street Journal* Bestselling Author Susan Stoker has a heart as big as the state of Tennessee where she lives, but this all American girl has also spent the last fourteen years living in Missouri, California, Colorado, Indiana, and Texas. She's married to a retired Army man who now gets to follow *her* around the country.

www.stokeraces.com
www.AcesPress.com
susan@stokeraces.com

Made in the USA
Coppell, TX
17 June 2021

57612524R00149